An unforgettable Hollywood princess in a small Southern town,
Divine Matthews-Hardison
lights up Jacquelin Thomas's previous novels

DIVINE CONFIDENTIAL

"There's something compelling about Divine and her amusing take on
life."
—*Booklist*

SIMPLY DIVINE

"Jacquelin Thomas has created entertaining characters that you care
about, in a page-turning story that's sure to touch lives."
—ReShonda Tate Billingsley, *Essence*
bestselling author of *The Pastor's Wife*

"*Simply Divine* is down-to-earth and heavenly minded all at the same
time. . . . It made me laugh and tear up."
—Nicole C. Mullen, Grammy-nominated and
Dove Award–winning vocalist

More acclaim for the wonderful faith-based fiction
of Jacquelin Thomas

"Touching and refreshing."
—*Publishers Weekly*

"Bravo! . . . Sizzles with the glamour of the entertainment industry and
real people who struggle to find that precious balance between their
drive for success and God's plan for their lives."
—Victoria Christopher Murray

"A fast-paced, engrossing love story . . . [with] Christian principles."
—*School Library Journal*

"Entertaining."
—*Booklist*

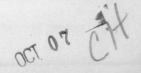

ALSO BY JACQUELIN THOMAS

Simply Divine
Divine Confidential

divine secrets

Jacquelin Thomas

POCKET BOOKS

New York   London   Toronto   Sydney

Pocket Books
A Division of Simon & Schuster, Inc.
1230 Avenue of the Americas
New York, NY 10020

Copyright © 2007 by Jacquelin Thomas

First Pocket Books trade paperback edition October 2007

POCKET and colophon are registered trademarks of Simon & Schuster, Inc.

For information about special discounts for bulk purchases, please contact Simon & Schuster Special Sales at 1-800-456-6798 or business@simonandschuster.com

Manufactured in the United States of America

10 9 8 7 6 5 4 3 2 1

Library of Congress Cataloging-in-Publication Data

Thomas, Jacquelin.
    Divine secrets / Jacquelin Thomas.
        p.   cm.
    Summary: While Hollywood teenager Divine Matthews-Hardison is staying in Georgia with her devoutly Christian uncle and his family, she faces difficult choices about keeping secrets that might be harmful to others, and how—or whether—to accept her mother's boyfriend into her life.
    [1. Family problems—Fiction. 2. Secrets—Fiction. 3. African Americans—Fiction. 4. Christian life—Fiction. 5. Georgia—Fiction.] I. Title.
PZ7.T366932Di 2007
[Fic]—dc22   2007026902

ISBN-13: 978-1-4165-5144-7
ISBN-10:   1-4165-5144-1

For all survivors of domestic violence
Love doesn't have to hurt

acknowledgments

As always, I have to thank my Heavenly Father for my gift of writing. With Him, all things are possible.

I have to thank my family for their constant unwavering support. I love you all.

I'd like to acknowledge and thank the many domestic violence organizations for taking time to answer my questions and provide information during the writing of this novel. I couldn't have done this without the following:

Center for the Prevention of School Violence
National Domestic Violence Hotline
National Center for Victims of Crime
Family Violence Prevention Center
National Resource Center on Domestic Violence

Deepening friendships mean people can trust you with their secrets, both large and small. Good friends never break a confidence—at least that's what we've always been taught . . .

chapter 1

"*Alyssa,* how am I supposed to get my dance on with Uncle Reed and Aunt Phoebe guard-dogging us all night long?" Sighing loudly, I throw my hands up in resignation, acting like a total drama queen. "I change my mind. I'm not going to the Sweethearts' Dance," I say, referring to the dance always held the Saturday before Valentine's Day.

"I can't have your mom and dad watching me like a hawk. Talk about total humiliation. If I wanted a bodyguard, I could call Leo and have him go to the dance with us. At least with him we'd look cool."

The more I think about it, the more I like the idea. Leo was my dad's best friend and was employed as his bodyguard before Jerome went to prison.

"You really need to chill," Alyssa replies while checking her

1

reflection in the full-length mirror standing in the corner of my bedroom. "My parents aren't just gonna be watching us. They have to keep their eyes on all the students."

"How much do you wanna bet?" I huff. "Aunt Phoebe and Uncle Reed have a vested interest in us. I'm telling you . . . girl, it's going to be all about us."

Tearing herself from my mirror finally, Alyssa asks, "A *what* kind of interest?"

She's standing there with this ugly frown on her face. I just love using the new words I learn daily in sentences because it drives my cousins, Alyssa and Chance, crazy and it makes me seem much smarter than they are. "*Vested.* It means protected or established by law, commitment, tradition, or ownership."

Alyssa shakes her head, her microbraids swinging back and forth. "We *have* to go to the dance, Divine. Everybody is gonna be there. And we get to go with dates. *Girl, we're actually getting to go out with Stephen and Madison.* How long have we been waiting for that to happen? It's a miracle."

"Well, I didn't expect *your parents* to be there with us," I complain, checking myself out in the oval, full-length mirror standing near the window. My new razor-cut, shoulder-length hairstyle is holding up well and looks great. "This sucks big-time. I can see it now . . . Madison and I start slow-dancing and here comes Uncle Reed measuring to see if we're too close—no body parts touching. I bet we won't be able to walk outside to get some air without Aunt Phoebe hot on our tails. How can they embarrass us like this?"

"At least they're letting us go to the dance. Divine, you know how my dad feels about stuff like this," Alyssa tells me. "If it weren't for Mama talking him into letting us go, we'd be staying home tonight. So let's just go and have a good time with our boyfriends."

"Madison and I are not together," I quickly correct her. "We're just friends."

Alyssa chuckles. "Yeah, right. You know Madison is your boo."

I break into a grin because she's right. A warm feeling spreads through my body at just the mention of Madison Hartford's name. He has his name all over my heart. "I'm taking my time with him. Like I'm not about to let him think he can just come running back to me whenever he feels like it. That brotha is gonna have to work hard to get me back."

Picking up my comb, I style my flat-ironed hair, then check my makeup. Aunt Phoebe only lets me wear lip gloss and powder foundation. But I'm not tripping because I still look fierce. I have what my mom calls inner beauty. "It's gonna be some hatin' going on tonight when we walk into the dance."

"Girl . . . wait till Stephen and Madison see us. They're going to lose their minds over how cute we're looking tonight."

I totally agree. My cousin and I really look hot in our dresses. Mom bought them in Los Angeles and sent them two weeks ago. They actually look more sophisticated than some of the dresses she's bought us before—more grown-up. Even Aunt Phoebe with her no kind of fashion sense managed to find the perfect purse and shoes to match Alyssa's red dress and my white one.

We'd arranged to meet Stephen and Madison at the school. Uncle Reed had suggested they ride with us, but I wasn't having it. It would be too lame to pull up in a car with our dates and my aunt and uncle.

I don't want to be late, so I say to Alyssa, "Hurry up. We need to get going."

Alyssa takes another look in the mirror. "Okay, I'm ready."

We walk out of my bedroom and head up to the front of the house where Aunt Phoebe and Uncle Reed are waiting for us.

For once, my aunt actually listened to me and decided on wearing the red suit with the silver trim. It looks good on her—Aunt Phoebe can come out of the box when it comes to fashion. I'm trying to work with her, but it's so hard sometimes. Especially since she's six feet tall. I'm a trendsetter and prone to showing off my unique sense of style, while my aunt Phoebe would be buried somewhere under the jail by the fashion police.

At about five-eight, Uncle Reed is a conservative dresser. He just looks like a preacher all the time, and he probably owns more black suits than anyone else in the world. At least he's wearing a red tie tonight. I have a teddy bear that looks just like him, down to the wire-framed glasses.

"You girls ready?" Aunt Phoebe asks, checking us out. "Oh, you both look beautiful."

"Thank you," we reply in unison.

I'm as ready as I can be with my aunt and uncle coming to the dance with us. They are so messing up my style. I admit I got in over my head that one time when I met the psycho over the internet, but this time it's different.

It's just a dance.

ON THE SHORT drive to the school, I think about my cousin Chance and his girlfriend Trina. They're not going to the dance tonight because he has to work and Trina is due to deliver their baby around the end of March. She's been dealing with a lot of swelling and feeling sick, so her parents are keeping her home until the baby comes. She's on independent study right now.

I'm still tripping over the fact that Chance and Trina are really having a baby next month. My aunt and uncle were totally upset at first, but now everyone is all excited. I guess they had no choice but to accept it because the baby's coming anyway. Uncle Reed is a preacher and says sex before marriage is a sin. He and Aunt Phoebe were disappointed because their own son wasn't listening when it came to that. Uncle Reed probably thinks that other people won't listen to him if his own children mess up. Personally, I don't think it's their fault at all. Teenagers are going to try stuff no matter what sometimes. It's not right, but it's just being a teen. To be honest, I'm not exactly thrilled to have a crying baby in the house. But then again, it's not like this is my real home—it feels like it is, but it's not.

Uncle Reed parks the car near the gym where the dance is being held. Alyssa climbs out, looking around for Stephen and Madison. They're supposed to be meeting us right out front. I get out of the car, checking out the surroundings, too.

It's cold outside and I'm not about to freeze standing out here waiting on Madison. I can't believe they're late. We'll look all crazy walking into the dance by ourselves. I'm not going out like that. I'll go back home first.

Stephen walks out through the front doors of the school with Madison following him. I release a soft sigh of relief.

My boo is here.

Aunt Phoebe pauses long enough to tell us, "I expect you both to act like young ladies. Once you walk inside this school—y'all better stay inside until we're ready to leave. We ain't having no funny bizness going on. *I mean it.*"

A couple of kids walking by us pause long enough to hear Aunt Phoebe's mouth and start to giggle. I'm so wanting to die of embarrassment. Now would be a really good time for Aunt Phoebe to catch a bad case of laryngitis.

Just before we walk inside, my semi-best-friend Mia and her boyfriend show up. She looks pretty in the red leather pantsuit she's wearing, but Tim . . . oh my gosh . . . he's looking all thuggish.

His pants are hanging so low, they look like they're about to fall off his tail, and he's got a bandanna tied around his braids. I wonder if he knows that his fashion risk actually started in prison. It's how prisoners advertise their willingness to have sex with another inmate.

Jerome told me that even before he went to prison. He had

never been a fan of baggy pants and oversize shirts. I used to think the look was cool until I found out where the style originated.

We wait for them to catch up and make our grand entrance together.

I steal a peek at the boy Mia's been seeing for the last three or four months. He's kind of cute. I don't know what it is exactly, but I don't really like Tim. It's just something about him that doesn't feel right to me. He doesn't say a whole lot when he's at school— just walks around with an attitude all the time. He only seems to kick it with the boys that stay in trouble all the time for fighting or skipping school and smoking weed.

"Divine, you wearing that dress, gurl," Mia complimented. "You look hot."

I smile at the compliment. "You do, too."

I feel Tim's gaze on me and glance up. He's just standing there staring at me, a shadow of annoyance hovering in his eyes.

Feeling uncomfortable, I turn to Madison and say, "I feel like dancing."

My boo's so into me that he doesn't notice the sudden tension in the air. Grinning, he takes my hand and leads me to the dance floor.

On the dance floor, I allow the music to sweep me up and carry me away with the rhythm. I love music and I love to dance. Alyssa and Stephen follow us, and soon the four of us are dancing and singing to Yung Joc's song "It's Goin' Down."

I hold back from showing off some of the dance moves I learned off BET because hawkeye Aunt Phoebe is standing near the edge of the dance floor, checking us out hard.

I wish she'd go get a life.

Mia and Tim navigate through the crowd, finding us. We dance through three more songs. I need a minute to make sure I'm not looking whack, so Madison and I leave the dance floor. He takes a seat at our table while I make a bathroom run. Alyssa and Mia join me there a few minutes later.

"I didn't know Stephen could dance like that," Alyssa says. "My boo can really dance."

I laugh. "He's okay . . . Did you see Nicholas out there? Now, I didn't know he had any rhythm outside of typing on a keyboard." He's a good friend of mine, but the boy is a major nerd.

Penny and Stacy walk into the bathroom giggling about something.

"It's about time y'all got here," Alyssa says.

"It was Penny. You know she always late for everything." Stacy pulls a brush out of her purse and makes an attempt to tame her hair. She has curls flying all over the place. I have no idea what she's trying to do, but in my opinion—it definitely didn't work. "That music's sounding good. I'ma get my party on," she tells us.

"Did I really see Aunt Phoebe and Uncle Reed out there?" Penny questions while touching up her lipstick.

"Yeah," I respond. "Our bodyguards are here."

Mia laughs along with Stacy and Penny, leading Alyssa to pinch me on the arm and say, "You need to not be talking about my parents like that."

"Like you're happy about them being here," I respond. "You were just as upset about it when you first found out, Alyssa."

"They're here and there's nothing we can do about it. *Let it go, Divine.*"

I take a step back when Alyssa tosses her braids over her shoulder. "Hey, watch it . . . you're dangerous with those things."

"I love my braids. I'll probably wear my hair like this forever."

"That's a bold statement. Fashion risk and all. Not to mention what it might do to your hair."

"Don't hate," Alyssa responds with a grin.

We stand around in the bathroom talking about everything—from boys to makeup to curfews. After chatting for a little over ten minutes, we walk out to reunite with our dates.

"What took you so long?" Tim demands as soon as we return to the table. "I'm sitting here waitin' on you."

I glance over at Mia, who suddenly looks like she's scared of the boy. She's over there stuttering and stuff trying to explain that we took a little girl time for ourselves. What's up with that?

Madison strokes my arm, bringing my attention back to him. "You look good," he whispers in my ear. "Right now I just want to kiss those sweet lips of yours."

I giggle until Aunt Phoebe's tall Amazon self walks over to the table. She gives me this funny look before asking, "Y'all behaving yourselves?"

"Mama . . . ," Alyssa groans.

"I'm just checking," Aunt Phoebe responds before moving on to the next table.

I glance over at Mia, who's in what still looks like an intense conversation with Tim. I drop my eyes when he glances my way.

Madison stands up and grabs my hand. "C'mon, let's dance. I like this song."

Holding hands, we make our way to the center of the dance floor. Madison and I move to the beat, looking fierce as can be. I bet we're the best-looking couple here.

Just as we make it back to the table, Tim rushes to his feet, pulling Mia with him. Mia plasters on a fake smile and practically whispers to me, "I'll s-see y'all later."

"You're leaving?" I ask.

She nods. "Tim's ready to go. I'll call you tomorrow."

Tim grunts something to her and Mia looks like she's about to cry.

What is going on between them? I wonder. I do know one thing—I'd never let the thug talk to me any kind of way. Humph.

He wouldn't punk me like that.

"WHAT'S UP WITH that fool?" Madison asks when Tim and Mia leave.

I shrug. "He's a real jerk. Can you believe he got upset just because we went to the bathroom? *That's crazy.*"

Madison reaches over and takes my hand in his. I quickly search the room to see where my aunt and uncle are—I don't need them tripping. He leans forward to steal a kiss.

"They're on the other side of the room talking to the principal," he whispers. "It's Valentine's Day and I miss kissing you."

I check out the room one more time because I've been missing Madison's lips, too. I'd never admit it to him though.

We kiss, sending the pit of my stomach into a wild swirl.

"Y'all better cut that out," Alyssa warns. "My mom and dad will be checking on us soon. You know they usually show up around now."

"Chill, Alyssa," I respond. "It was just a little kiss. It's not like we were in a lip-lock."

"Tell it to my parents when they catch you. Personally, I don't care what you and Madison do, but I'm not getting in trouble with you."

"Like we have anything to worry about," I respond. "Nobody saw us."

No sooner have the words slipped out of my mouth, Aunt Phoebe and Uncle Reed walk up to our table. I scan their faces to see if I can get a heads-up on if I'm busted or not.

I steal a glance over at Alyssa, who looks like she's been caught with her hand in the cookie jar. I think she's trying to tell me something, but I can't figure it out.

Uncle Reed asks, "Where is Mia and her date?"

"They left," Madison answers.

"Son, you might want to wipe off that lip gloss," Uncle Reed tells him. "You look like you've been eating pork chops."

Stephen and Alyssa burst into laughter while I hand my boo a napkin.

Aunt Phoebe places a hand on my shoulder, leans down, and whispers, "Keep those lips of yours to yourself, sugar. *Understand me?*"

I can feel my face growing warm. "Yes, ma'am."

Right now I'm hating Uncle Reed for calling Madison out like that. My aunt and uncle truly suck.

I let out a long sigh when they move on to the next table. I can't believe they just did that to us.

"You got busted," Alyssa says with a laugh as if I didn't have a clue. I'm the one sitting over here flaming with embarrassment.

"Shut up," I snap.

My revenge comes later when Uncle Reed walks onto the dance floor to pry Alyssa and Stephen apart. I howl with laughter. My cousin looks like she's about to pass out in her humiliation.

Back at the table, Alyssa pinches my arm.

"Hey, that hurts."

"That's for laughing at me."

"You should've seen your face." I chuckle. "I thought you were gonna die right on the spot."

"To be honest . . . I thought I was, too. I thought Mama was gonna take me out right on that dance floor. I can't believe she embarrassed me like that."

We decide to sit at our table talking for the rest of the evening. Especially since the deejay is playing a lot of slow songs.

Five minutes past one a.m., Aunt Phoebe comes to the table and announces, "We're getting ready to leave. Say your good-byes and meet us at the car."

I glance over at Madison. "I guess I'll give you a call tomorrow. We're going to Atlanta to see my mom."

"Put your phone on vibrate. I'ma call you later."

"Okay. If I don't answer right away, call me back. I know Aunt Phoebe's going to want to fuss."

Alyssa interrupts us. "Mama and Daddy just walked out. We better get out there. I don't feel like being embarrassed any more tonight."

Sighing in resignation, I pick up my leather coat and slip it on, thinking it would've been better to just stay home than to have to live down the humiliation of having to leave with my aunt and uncle as soon as the lights come on. We barely have any time to say good-bye to our friends.

Parents can be so mean.

It's times like these that I consider going back to live with my mom. But with my dad in prison and Mom starring in movies and recording a new album, I don't have a stable home environment— not like I do with Aunt Phoebe and Uncle Reed. With them I feel like I have a normal life.

And a curfew.

chapter 2

As soon as we walk into the house, Aunt Phoebe calls us into the family room for a lecture. I already know it's going to be about me and Madison kissing. It was only *one* kiss. Like what's the big deal?

"Did you two have fun tonight?" she asks when we take a seat on the sofa.

"Yes, ma'am," we respond in unison.

I can't help but feel like she's being just a little too nice. Aunt Phoebe's setting us up before she moves in for the kill.

"Until we had to leave early in front of everybody," I add. "That was so embarrassing."

Aunt Phoebe stares me down. "But I'm sure you appreciate going to the dance even though you left an hour early. Right?"

"Yes, ma'am." She's narrowing in on us. I can feel it.

"It looked to us like you and Alyssa were enjoying your-selves."

I wait for Aunt Phoebe to continue. I know it's coming. She always has something to say about everything.

"Divine, your uncle and I know how much you like Madison, but we think it's best if you don't do anything to get yourself in trouble. One kiss leads to another, and before you know it—you're naked and don't know how you got there."

Heat steals into my face. "Aunt Phoebe," I sputter. "I'm not about to be naked with anybody."

"You can't control your emotions, sugar. You couldn't even keep your lips off that boy tonight."

Embarrassed, I don't respond. There's not a whole lot I can say at this point. She's definitely got me there.

Uncle Reed speaks up. "Think about what I'm about to say. There are only two states of romantic involvement outlined in the Bible—singleness and marriage. There is no room in between for physical interaction. *Right?* In fact, the Bible tells us that it is a sin to fornicate."

"Yes, sir," Alyssa and I both answer. I can't believe he's about to preach to us this late. Why can't he just wait until Sunday and put us on blast?

"So what does that say to you?"

"It tells me that if you're not married, don't touch. But if you are married, you can go hog wild like Aunt Phoebe says."

Alyssa chuckles.

"I wouldn't have put it in those terms," Uncle Reed tells me, "but you're right."

"We understand what you and Mama are saying," Alyssa states. "It's not like we're having sex. I'm waiting until I get married, and you know Divine's all proud about being the big '*V*.' We have all these feelings that God gave us, and sometimes it's frustrating.

Stephen and I really care for each other, and I know you don't want to hear that, but it's true. If he and I were just friends, y'all wouldn't care if he came to the house. But because he's my boyfriend . . . just because we hold hands, you and Mama get upset. We're not doing anything and it's frustrating to have all these feelings for a person and not really be able to explore them."

"She's right," I interject. "I feel the same way. Right now, I'm sitting here feeling like I've done something really terrible, but it was only one kiss. I used to see Mom and Jerome kissing all the time. I see you and Uncle Reed kiss. I know you're married and all, but I haven't seen anywhere in the Bible that says kissing is wrong. I admit I haven't read the entire book either, but why did God give teens all these emotions if we can't control them?"

"God also gave you parents to help you rein them in," Aunt Phoebe responds. "Sugar, you don't know just how scary it is for us as parents during this time of your lives. Having a teen that is on the verge of love and lust . . . Lord, have mercy . . ."

"Is it that bad, Aunt Phoebe?" I ask with a chuckle.

She breaks into a grin. "It's not a bad thing, but it's not an easy time either. Our challenge is helping you deal with those emotions. A parent's goal should be to allow young adolescents to embrace love but to give them guidance in how to handle lust and remain abstinent."

"Mama, do you feel like you failed because of Chance?"

I can't believe Alyssa just asked her mom that. Still, I'd like to know the answer myself. I chew on my bottom lip while waiting on her response.

"Initially, I did," Aunt Phoebe admits. "I wondered if I'd said enough—if I'd done enough—but then I had to come to the realization that all we as parents can do is give you the information. Ultimately, the choice is yours to make."

"It's the same with God," Uncle Reed tells us. "He's given us the information—His Word. It's up to us to follow Him or the world."

"Aunt Phoebe, you've done a wonderful job with us," I assure her. "You, too, Uncle Reed. You don't have to worry so much about us."

"Oh, but we do," Aunt Phoebe counters. "It's because we love y'all so much. And this world is sometimes much too enticing to pass up—not just for young people. For everyone. We just want y'all to stay grounded in the Word and in prayer. Always ask yourself, what would Jesus do?"

We talk a few minutes more on the dos and don'ts of dating before Alyssa and I are allowed to go to our rooms.

I get ready for bed.

Madison calls me on my cell phone.

"I just wanted to say good-night," he tells me.

I laugh. "Stop lying. You just called to see if I got into any trouble."

"Did you?"

"No. Not really. We had another talk about dating dos and don'ts. Parents are convinced they know everything—that's something that'll never change."

It'll always be that way.

Mɪᴀ ᴄᴀʟʟs ᴍᴇ first thing Saturday morning. After the way she and Tim left so abruptly last night, I had a feeling I'd be hearing from her.

"Mia, hold on," I say. I lay the phone down on the counter in my bathroom long enough to pull my towel tight around my body. I'd just gotten out of the shower when my cell started jumping around due to the vibration.

I secure my wireless headset on my ear. "Okay, I can talk while I get dressed. I leave for my tae kwon do class in a few minutes."

"You really like taking that?"

"Yeah. I'm working on getting my blue belt."

"Which means what?"

"That I'm reaching higher. My instructor says, it's like a plant reaching for the sky." Changing the subject, I ask, "Why did you and Tim leave so early?"

"He was ready to go. Tim doesn't like crowds much."

"Did you guys make up? It looked like the two of you were fighting before you left."

"We straightened everything out when we got back to my house. Tim just thought I'd left him alone too long. He said that Madison and Stephen were basically ignoring him, and he didn't like sitting at a table with people dissing him."

"They weren't dissing him," I say.

"You don't know that. You were in the bathroom with us. A lot of the boys at school don't like Tim."

"Hmmm . . . I wonder why?"

There's a click on the other end. Someone's trying to reach Mia. She ignores it.

"I think they're scared of Tim."

"Who?" I'd like to know. He doesn't scare me, that's for sure.

We keep talking while I slip into a pair of jeans and an embellished sweatshirt.

"So did anything good happen after we left?"

"Katrina Hamilton and Michele Taylor almost came to blows over T.J. My uncle made Katrina leave since she was the one who started the argument in the first place. I don't know why she keeps bothering Michele."

"What was T.J. doing?"

"Standing around like the rest of us just watching them argue," I respond. "He didn't even come with Katrina or Michele. That's why they both looked stupid. T.J. is trying to go with Linda Carter. He's always up in her face."

"I heard Katrina's pregnant for him," Mia announces. "That's probably why she's acting so crazy."

"I hope for her sake that she isn't."

"I don't know, but I heard she's at least four months pregnant."

"Who is blowing up your phone?" I question when I hear that irritating click for the eighth or ninth time.

"It's Tim. Hold on."

"Mia, wait—"

No, she didn't just put me on hold for that boy. I told her I have to leave soon.

Mia clicks back saying, "Divine, I need to call you back."

She sounds upset so I ask, "What's wrong?"

"I'll call you back."

Before I can respond that I'm about to walk out of the house, Mia hangs up. She totally needs to dump that jerk.

I make a mental note to tell her just that when I speak to her later. I can't believe he acted so rude last night at the dance. Everybody was having a good time and there he was—just sitting there acting all bored. Then he's got the nerve to tell Mia that Madison and Stephen were dissing him. He's the one with the attitude.

I shake my head. Mia can do so much better than Tim.

My cell phone rings just as I get into the car with Chance. He's dropping me off at my class since it's on his way to work.

Seeing Mia's name on the caller ID, I quickly answer. "Hey, girl. Mia, what's up with you and Tim? Last night, it looked like you were upset and then when you got off the phone earlier."

"We got into an argument because he thought I was ignoring him."

"*What?* Why would he think that? Like you were sitting right next to the boy the whole night." I shake my head, saying, "He's seriously tripping."

"Tim likes a lot of attention. That's all."

"I hope you don't get mad at me for saying this, because you're my girl and all . . . Mia, I just don't think he's the guy for you."

She sighs softly before replying, "Divine, you don't know him. He's a good guy. Just moody sometimes. Tim don't like crowds much."

"That's going to put a damper on his partying," I mumble. "You love being around a group of people, Mia. How are you two going to work this out?"

"We're okay now, Divine. Tim just wanted to leave last night." Mia changes the subject when she asks, "So what are you and Alyssa doing later on today?"

"We're leaving for Atlanta. My mom is in town. Alyssa and I are spending the night there and we'll be back in time for church tomorrow."

"That's nice. I bet y'all gon' have a good time."

"Why don't you come with us? My mom won't mind, Mia."

"I can't go. Tim is coming by the house this evening."

"What's that got to do with anything? It's not like you're married to the boy." I can't believe what I'm hearing out of Mia's mouth. She loves going to my mom's house in Atlanta. "I must have the wrong number because this sure don't sound like my friend. This is definitely not the Mia who loves going to Atlanta for any reason and who especially loves the indoor heated pool at my mom's house."

Mia breaks into a short laugh. "Divine, I like spending time with my boyfriend, too. *Okay?*"

"Whatever."

"Well, have a good time in Atlanta. Call me when you get back."

"I will." I can't believe my girl is going out like that. Mia used to break up with a boy if he didn't call her two days in a row. She didn't take no mess from anybody so it's hard for me to believe she's fooling around with that jerk Tim.

I don't know what's going on, but I totally intend to find out. Mia is a semi-BFF and I can't let her play herself. She can't have me going around looking like I have whack friends. I'm so not going out like that.

My friend Nicholas is standing outside the building when I arrive. He takes tae kwon do classes with me. "You were tearing up the dance floor last night," I say. "I didn't know you could move like that."

"I know you think I'm a nerd, but I got skills."

Laughing, we walk inside.

This morning we work on our sparring, called *Ryorugi,* for the competition.

After the hour-long class, Nicholas and I walk home together.

"Is Mia really going with that dude from Birmingham? Tim Mallory?"

"Yeah. I don't know why. There's something about him that I just don't like. He looks so mean."

"I heard he was in a gang."

"I can believe it," I say.

We change the subject, discussing our upcoming competition the rest of the way home. Nicholas leaves me at my house, then makes his way over one block to where he lives.

Inside the house, my cell phone rings again. This time it's Rhyann, my best friend in Los Angeles. "Hey, girl," I say when I answer.

"You've been in the South much too long," she complains. "You're starting to sound like your cousins."

"Whatever . . ."

"Did you have fun at the Sweethearts' Dance with Madison?"

"Yeah. We had a great time. How about you and Carson? Did you guys have fun at your dance? That's the one thing I do miss about Stony Hills Prep. The school dances."

"Girl, I danced all night. I was so tired when I got home," Rhyann says. "And you should have seen Mimi. The dress she was wearing was nice. I don't think I've ever seen her look so pretty."

"Really? Rhyann, did you take any pictures?"

"I did. I'll email them to you in a little while."

We talk for almost an hour, catching up since our last conversation two days ago.

Aunt Phoebe comes into my room. "Sugar, you need to get busy if you're going to your mama's house. You got chores to do before you go anywhere."

"I'll give you a call later," I tell Rhyann. My aunt really knows how to ruin a mood.

"I don't know how you put up with her."

"Bye, Rhyann." I practically hang up on her. I love my friend but I don't like her talking about my aunt. I don't play that mess. Besides, Rhyann goes through the same stuff I do, so I don't know what she's trying to say.

I leave my room in search of my aunt. "Aunt Phoebe, I've already cleaned my room and my laundry is done. What else do I need to do?"

"What about your bathroom? Have you cleaned it?"

I hate cleaning the bathroom. It's the absolute worst chore in the world. "Not yet."

"Have you cleaned your windows?"

"My windows," I repeat. "I have to clean windows?" This is the first I'm hearing of it.

Aunt Phoebe nods. "That's part of your room, isn't it?"

I'd never thought of it that way. "Aunt Phoebe, you never said anything about me cleaning any windows. I just assumed it was part of the house—like outside the house."

"The Windex is in the pantry."

"Aunt Phoebe, I'm telling you, we really should get a maid. It would make things so much easier. Look at what it's doing to me." I show her my fingernails. "These chores are ruining my nails. I need to have a manicure like every other day."

"Why do I need a maid when I got two good hands and a house full of healthy people?"

"Because you love me and you take pity on my poor hands. I can't be a fierce model with ugly hands, Aunt Phoebe. *It just won't work.*"

Instead of pity or even a mere hint of sympathy, I get laughter.

Life is so unfair.

Shortly after twelve, we leave for Atlanta.

"I hope Miss Eula made one of her lemon pound cakes," Alyssa states. "I have a taste for one so bad."

I laugh. Every time we visit my mom's house in Atlanta, Alyssa wants lemon pound cake. "I'm sure Miss Eula baked one," I tell my cousin. "She knows how much you like it."

Aunt Phoebe mutters something we don't understand and shifts her position in the front seat of the van.

"I don't think your mom appreciates you talking about Miss Eula's cake like that," I whisper.

Alyssa's eyes dart to Aunt Phoebe, then back to me. "You think she mad?" she mouths to me.

I shrug.

"Mama, I like your cakes, too," Alyssa blurts.

I smile and glance out the window when Aunt Phoebe responds, "Honey, you don't have to tell me that. If it's got sugar in it, you love it."

I slip my headphones over my ears and lean back against the

leather-cushioned seats, scanning the playlist on my iPod while Alyssa listens to hers.

I'm so glad that she's listening to music or one of her audio-books because I don't feel like listening to her talk nonstop all the way to Atlanta. It's bad enough I can still hear Aunt Phoebe's voice over my music.

My cell phone vibrates, alerting me to an incoming call. I check the caller ID.

It's my boo.

I let it go to voice mail since I'm in the van with my aunt and uncle. I don't like them listening to my conversations with Madison—trying to be all up in my business.

Don't parents have enough to worry about without getting all involved with their children's lives? Uncle Reed is always preaching about let go and let God.

Well . . .

As soon as we walk into the house, I catch a whiff of Miss Eula's delicious cooking. My stomach growls in response.

Mom rushes toward me with her arms outstretched. "Come here, baby girl."

I fall into her arms, grinning. "You act like you miss me," I tease.

"No, I haven't missed you at all," she responds with a chuckle. Mom places a kiss on my cheek. "I'm so glad you're here."

Mom smells so good. I inhale the floral scent of So Pretty de Cartier, her favorite perfume. As far as I'm concerned, I have the most beautiful mother in the world. She's even been nominated as one of the top ten in Hollywood.

She hugs Alyssa before greeting my aunt and uncle.

Alyssa and I take our things upstairs while Mom talks with Aunt Phoebe and Uncle Reed.

"I love this house," Alyssa tells me for the nine-hundredth time.

"Why don't you just move here?" I suggest. "Since you love it so much."

"Because I want to spend time with Stephen."

"You only see him at school. We're still not allowed to date." I follow Alyssa into the room she usually stays in when we're visiting Mom. "I'm still mad at Chance for messing that up for us."

Alyssa places her overnight bag on the overstuffed, burgundy-colored chair in her room. "Divine, you can't keep making Chance feel bad about Trina. I think he feels guilty enough already."

"I'm not trying to make him feel bad. I'm just stating facts. It's not my fault."

We go to my room next, where I drop off my backpack and duffel. Alyssa and I return downstairs.

"Aunt Kara, where's Mama and Daddy?" Alyssa asks when we enter the kitchen, where Kara and Miss Eula are preparing lunch.

"They're in their room," Mom responds.

I embrace Miss Eula. "I'm so hungry."

She laughs. "Hello to you, too. Is that how you greeting folks these days?"

"No, ma'am," I say. "I'm sorry, Miss Eula. It's just that you got this food smelling so good . . . all I can think about is eating."

Alyssa hugs Miss Eula, who asks me, "Why you starving so? Did you miss breakfast or somethin'?"

"I had a bowl of cereal this morning. I just have a taste for your cooking. You should be glad, Miss Eula."

"Honey, I am. I love for my babies to eat. I don't want you walking around looking like toothpicks. You need some meat on your bones. Be nice and round like me."

I laugh.

"What you laughing 'bout? I'm serious."

I love Miss Eula to death, but I'm not about to gain a lot of weight.

"So how was the dance last night?" Mom asks.

I glance over at Alyssa, who responds, "I had a good time."

"Aunt Phoebe and Uncle Reed chaperoned," I say.

Mom laughs. "That was nice of them."

Shrugging, I say, "I guess it depends on how you look at it."

"So are you saying you didn't have a good time because Reed and Phoebe were there?"

"I had a decent time."

"Decent," Aunt Phoebe utters when she enters the kitchen. "I'd say you had a pretty good old time. Kissing that boy anyway."

Mom's eyes travel to mine while I'm wishing the floor would just open up and swallow me. "Divine, you and Madison were kissing?"

"It was *one* kiss and I didn't kiss him—it was the other way around."

"If your lips were pressed to his, you was kissing just as hard as he was," Aunt Eula contributes.

"Aunt Phoebe, you didn't have to bust me out like that."

"If one kiss isn't a big deal like you keep telling me, what's the problem with your mama knowing about it?"

"I wanted to tell her myself. Besides, she knows that Madison and I have kissed before."

"The only thing that needs to come close to your mouth is food and drink," Miss Eula says. "Better leave those no-count boys alone."

"I'm not doing anything," I assure Miss Eula. "Madison and I are not even together."

"Then why were you kissing him?"

"It was a friendly kiss."

"Uh-huh . . ."

"Really, it was," I insist.

We sat down ten minutes later to a lunch of fried chicken, homemade biscuits, and potato salad.

Afterward, Aunt Phoebe and Uncle Reed settle into the family room with Mom and Miss Eula, leaving me and Alyssa to do the cleaning up.

I resist grumbling about it because we're going to the mall with Mom when we finish. She's promised to take us shopping, which is my absolute favorite thing to do. Uncle Reed's planning on going to see the Atlanta Hawks play the Los Angeles Lakers.

Since my mom is totally in Mom mode, I intend to punish her by spending lots of her money. I've been waiting on this Nanette Lepore outfit from Neiman Marcus. *I'm getting it today*.

"I can't wait to get to the mall. Mama said I could spend two hundred dollars on clothes."

"That'll get me one outfit if I'm lucky or it's on sale," I respond.

"We're not rich like you. Okay?"

I look over at Alyssa. "I didn't mean it that way. I was just saying."

"Even if I was rich—I wouldn't spend the kind of money you spend on clothes. It's ridiculous."

"I like nice clothes."

"So do I," Alyssa counters. "I can find some stuff that looks even better than all that designer stuff you always want. You even borrow some of my clothes."

"Okay, Alyssa. Let's do this. Instead of going to Neiman Marcus or Saks, you pick the stores and let's see what we can find. I was shooting to spend at least a thousand dollars of Mom's money, but I won't. I'll just ask for two hundred dollars and see what I can find." My Nanette Lepore outfit will have to wait.

"That's a deal."

Putting away the last dish, I regret making the deal with Alyssa. I feel like I'm going to be on the losing end somehow.

We leave for the mall half an hour later.

In the car, I say, "Alyssa wants to go to Lenox Square mall. Oh, and, Mom . . ." I pull at the neck of my sweatshirt. "I only need two hundred dollars."

Mom glances at me from her rearview mirror. "Really?"

Aunt Phoebe turns around in her seat. "Did I just hear you correctly?"

"Alyssa's only got two hundred to spend and so she's going to show me how to work it and still get some tight clothes. I'm not real optimistic though."

"Tell her mama. We do it all the time."

"This should be interesting," Mom murmurs. "My baby has very expensive tastes. I guess it's my fault."

Aunt Phoebe agrees. "It's definitely your fault. Remember when we used to make our own clothes?"

"I didn't do a very good job," Mom replies with a laugh. "You let me go out there thinking I was looking cute . . . I was a sight."

"They didn't look bad."

"Mom, I didn't know you could sew," I say.

"I can't. Phoebe is the one who could throw down. She had to redo a lot of my stuff."

Thinking about Aunt Phoebe's terrible sense of fashion, I immediately sympathize with my mom.

Mom quickly secures an empty parking space and turns off the car. We climb out of her Volvo SUV.

"So what store are we going to?" I ask Alyssa. "Abercrombie and Fitch? French Connection?"

"The Gap."

"They have some pretty nice stuff," I say. It's not exactly on my list of stores to shop in, but I'm going to give it a try. I don't expect to find a whole lot there. I have loads of jeans. Maybe something will jump out at me.

Inside the store, Alyssa heads straight to the clearance racks. I follow, already regretting my decision.

The first thing that catches my eye is a cropped cable-knit hoodie in heather gray. I check the price tag. "It's only twenty-nine dollars."

"Are you going to get it?"

I nod.

Mom brings over a pair of wool Bermuda shorts. "These are cute."

I take them from her. "I'm getting those, too."

Alyssa discovers a cropped wool jacket marked down to $30. I'm hatin' on her because she found it first. I already know I'm going to want to borrow it.

Forty-five minutes or so pass before we stroll up to the cash register, our arms filled with clothing.

Alyssa's purchases come to $198.23. Mine come to $215.67. I glance over at Alyssa, who says, "You did good for your first time."

"I can't believe I'm walking out with three pairs of pants and three tops—three whole outfits for under two hundred fifty dollars."

"I got two outfits and a jacket. I'm so happy. I've been wanting this jacket for a long time."

Aunt Phoebe finds a couple of sweaters to buy for herself.

"Now I like those," I tell her. "Aunt Phoebe, they have some pants in tall sizes. You might want to take a look at them."

Mom bites her bottom lip to keep from laughing.

"I'm buying all I'm gon' buy. Thank you anyway." After paying for her purchases, she tells me, "Don't think I didn't catch what you're trying to say. Cropped pants are in style."

"Cropped pants may be in style, but high-waters are not.

And those jumpsuits, Aunt Phoebe . . . c'mon now. It's time to give them up."

"Phoebe, you still wearing jumpsuits?" Mom asks.

"They still fit. They may be a little short, but people wear all kinds of stuff these days, so I figure I'm just as fashionable as the rest."

Mom, Alyssa, and I break into a round of laughter. Aunt Phoebe is too funny at times.

My mom wants to go over to Neiman Marcus, so we leave Lenox and head over to Phipps Plaza.

"Remember you can't buy anything," Alyssa tells me. "You were only supposed to spend two hundred dollars."

"You are so not the boss of me."

Before Alyssa can respond, her cell phone rings. It's Stephen. I catch up with Mom and Aunt Phoebe to give her some privacy.

"She must be on the phone with that boy," my aunt mutters.

I chuckle.

"I don't know why you're giggling. Soon as Madison calls, you hang on to his every word."

"Aunt Phoebe, I don't know how you and Uncle Reed ever got married," I say. "Y'all make it sound like such a sin that we like boys. I bet you acted just like us when you and Mom were growing up."

"She was boy crazy," Mom states. "I can't talk because I was the same way. And guess what? Our mothers felt the exact same way we feel now."

I try to sneak a couple of sweaters in with Mom's purchases, but Alyssa catches me and tries to guilt me out.

I resist with all of my might. I want these sweaters. Every girl with any fashion sense has to own a YaYa. After eyeing the new Young, Fabulous & Broke collection, I announce, "Okay, look . . . I can't do this. I can't just spend two hundred dollars. I tried and I failed. Mom, please, I love this hoodie dress."

Mom decides that if she buys me one, she has to buy Alyssa one as well. I don't care—it's one of those outfits that you just have to have.

When we're finally shopped out, we make our way back to the house. I hope Miss Eula has dinner ready because all this shopping has worked up an appetite.

chapter 3

Alyssa and I are stuck once again with cleaning the kitchen. I have no idea why my mom likes giving her housekeeper the weekends off. When I come here, I'd like to be able to escape having to do manual labor.

There have been several times where I long for the days when I never had to lift a finger and the word "chores" was foreign to me.

We have just finished putting away the dishes when the doorbell sounds. A few minutes later, I hear Kevin Nash's voice. What is he doing? Stalking my mom?

"Kevin's here," Alyssa announces.

"I know. I can hear him." I sigh in resignation. "He can't let us have *one* weekend together. He's always here at the house."

"Why don't you like Kevin?" Alyssa wants to know. "He's nice."

"He's okay. I just don't like him hanging around my mom so much. They're just supposed to be friends."

Her gaze meets mine. "You think she's lying?"

I shrug. "They're always together. The tabloids are saying that they're a couple."

"You know better than anybody that you can't believe everything the tabloids say."

I nod in agreement, but deep down I'm not so sure. I know what Mom tells me, but the pictures I see in magazines and in the tabloids—they tell a different story.

I can hear Mom laughing at one of Kevin's lame jokes. Even Aunt Phoebe and Uncle Reed are cracking up. From what I hear, it isn't that funny.

Alyssa and I join them.

Greeting us, Kevin gives me a hug, then gives Alyssa one.

"I have something for the two of you," he says. "I bought it when I was in China a couple of weeks ago."

Now he's trying to buy his way into the family. Well, it's not going to work with me, I decide. Still, I'm curious as to what he bought me, so I ask, "What is it?"

"Divine . . ."

I glance over at Mom. "I was just asking."

"Just wait and see," she tells me.

Whatever . . .

Mom's eyes are still glued to my face; her expression almost leads me to believe she can hear my thoughts.

Kevin places a hand on her shoulder. "I'm a bit impatient when it comes to gifts myself."

I roll my eyes heavenward. Kevin really gets on my nerves. I wish I could knock his hand down, but my mom would knock me into the next year. I just don't think he has any right to touch her.

"Divine, I left the presents in the living room," Kevin announces. "You and Alyssa can go on and get your gifts."

I give him a tiny smile. "Thanks."

Alyssa and I take off. We love presents.

"What do you think it is?" Alyssa asks, holding up a small box.

"Some kind of jewelry. Like we need more of that."

"You can never have enough jewelry." Alyssa tears off the silver wrapping to get to a medium-size velvet box. Opening it, her eyes get as big as saucers. "Divine, it's beautiful. Look."

"It's jade," I tell her. The necklace is nice and comes with a matching bracelet and earrings. "It's pretty."

"Open yours."

"Kevin probably bought me the same thing." Jade's nice and all, but I already have enough of it.

I open my gift to find a tiger-eye necklace with matching earrings and bracelet. I absolutely love my gift, but I'm not about to show my true feelings to Kevin. I don't want him to think that he's made inroads with me.

We take them into the family room to show everyone.

"Thank you, Kevin," I say. Alyssa thanks him, too, only she's over there being all mushy. He's won her over for sure. Sorry, but he can't buy me that easily.

Mom reaches over and fingers the bracelets on my arm. "Your bracelets are so cute," Mom says. "Where on earth did you find them?"

"I designed them myself."

I laugh at the expression on my mom's face.

"Honey, you really made these?"

"Yes, ma'am. I designed them. Alyssa has her own line of jewelry, too. She mostly does earrings and necklaces though. I do the bracelets. We've even made some money off some of our creations. When I retire from modeling, I'm going to design jewelry."

Mom breaks into a smile. "That's right, baby girl. Always have a backup plan." She takes one of the bracelets I offer to her, inspecting it closely. "You did a beautiful job, sweetie. Show me everything you two ladies have and I'll purchase some."

"Aunt Kara, you don't have to pay for an—"

I interrupt quickly. "Alyssa, hush . . . we're tying to have a business, remember. We can't go giving our product away. Not even to family. If we do, then everybody will be wanting free jewelry."

"We can at least offer a discount, right?"

I think about it a moment before saying, "Yeah, I guess we can offer a family discount—key word being 'family,' Alyssa. *Immediate family only.* I know how you are."

Mom shakes her head and laughs.

Kevin decides to jump into our conversation by saying, "I'd like to purchase some of your jewelry for my family."

"Why?" I ask.

"You're in the jewelry business, right? Well, I have a couple of teenage nieces that I'm sure would love to have some of your bracelets and whatever else you have. They love jewelry."

I'm not crazy about Kevin, but I will take his money. "Each bracelet is ten dollars."

"I thought you were charging five dol—"

I cut Alyssa off. "They're ten dollars," I state, hoping she'll get the hint and shut up.

Mom can't even sit down without Kevin being right beside her. He's acting like a lovesick puppy. I frown in disgust.

He pulls out his wallet, but Mom stops him. "You've been so generous—I'd like to buy the bracelets for your nieces."

How can she betray me like that? She's sitting over there glaring at me like I've done something wrong. I'm totally not feeling her right now.

"I'm going to my room," I announce suddenly. As if somebody really cares. They are so in love with Kevin, they probably won't even notice that I'm leaving.

Standing, I cross the room in quick strides, making my way to the spiral staircase. I slow my pace just a little to see if Mom or Aunt Phoebe—someone—calls me back.

They don't.

Mad at the world, I stomp up the stairs.

"Girl, what's wrong with you?" Alyssa demands when she comes to my room a few minutes later. "Why are you tripping? And since when did you start charging ten dollars?"

"Didn't you see the way Kevin was acting? He was all over my mom," I fume.

Alyssa makes herself at home on my bed. "He likes Aunt Kara. I don't know why you think that's so bad. Divine, you should be happy your mom's found a good man. And he's real nice to you. He's trying to be your friend."

"Kevin is way too old to be my friend. He's just nice to me because he wants my mom. After he gets her—all that will change. I've seen it happen with some of my friends. They get shipped to boarding school right after the wedding."

"You live with us, so I don't think you have to worry about boarding school, Divine. Besides, Aunt Kara wouldn't go for that. You told me that you asked to go when you were in the fifth grade and she said no."

"It's not boarding school that bothers me."

"Then what is it?"

"Alyssa, I still remember how she used to be with Jerome. She wasn't happy—she was stressed all the time and they did nothing but argue. You know that's when she started doing drugs. I love my mom the way she is now."

"You really think Aunt Kara will go back to doing drugs?"

I shrug. "I don't know. She and Jerome didn't have a healthy relationship—her words, not mine. How do we know if Kevin is healthy for her?"

"Divine, I think you're just going to have to trust Aunt Kara. She's grown and can do whatever she wants to, and that includes dating Kevin Nash. That man is so fine—he could be my stepfather for sure."

I make a face. "Then *you* take him. I just want Mom to keep their relationship friendly with no 'touchy-feely' stuff. She doesn't need a boyfriend—she has me."

"What you two gals doing in here?" Miss Eula inquires from the doorway. "I know you plotting something."

"We're just talking, Miss Eula."

She ambles all the way into the bedroom, saying, "I came up here to see if you wanted to include a letter to your daddy. I'm fixing to send him a care package. That boy is like a son to me and I miss him so much."

"Could you just tell Jerome I said hello?"

"I could, but I think he'd really appreciate it coming directly from you. You can put your letter in the envelope with mine."

I know Miss Eula well enough to know that she isn't going to just let this go, so I tell her, "Okay, I'll write him one tonight."

"Leave it downstairs on the kitchen counter and I'll get it in the morning. I want to send the package out first thing Monday morning."

"Yes, ma'am."

"By the way, you might want to try being a little nicer to Kevin. He's an all right guy and he really cares for your mama."

"I didn't do anything," I say. "Why is everybody on my case?"

"Like I told you—try and be a little nicer." Miss Eula rises to her feet, sighing loudly. "Lawd, I'm tired. I'm gonna call it a night. I'll see y'all in the morning. Don't y'all stay up too late talking. You gotta get up early 'cause your uncle say he pulling out at eight a.m. sharp."

"Miss Eula thinks she's my other mom," I say when she leaves the room. "I got her, Aunt Phoebe . . . Mom . . . I sure hope Ava isn't trying to get in here because I don't have any more room when it comes to mothering. I know she's Jerome's wife and all, but I have way too many as is."

Alyssa laughs.

"Don't you ever feel this way?"

She nods. "Sometimes. But that's just the way it is when people care about you."

"I'm glad they care, but there are times I wish they didn't care so much. I guess that makes me ungrateful."

"I know what you mean. You want to be able to make decisions about your own life."

"I know that I still have a lot to learn, but isn't that why we make mistakes—so we can learn from them? We're supposed to be gaining experience. If we're locked up at home, how can we experience anything?"

"I guess it's because sometimes we risk getting into some serious trouble."

I nod in agreement. "Like when I ran off to meet Theopolis Mack. That could've turned out real ugly—like me being dead. I'm not ever going to do anything so totally stupid again."

"I've made some bad choices, too. The thing is, Divine, we're not bad people. I mean we're not perfect either. I still tell a lie or two—"

I laugh. "Or two? Girl . . ."

"Hey, I only tell lies to stay out of trouble. I'm not out trying to hurt people."

"You think God's going to care why you lied? I don't think so. Uncle Reed says sin is sin." I pick up a pillow and hold it close to my heart. "You know what, Alyssa? I actually have a problem with that. If Uncle Reed is right, then my sins weigh the same as a serial killer's. Like that'll suck big-time if I go to heaven and the first person I see is Theopolis Mack after all he's done. I read that he's suspected of murdering at least ten girls." I met Theopolis Mack online, only I thought he was a sixteen-year-old boy named Sean. I made the stupid mistake of sneaking out to meet him a few months ago and he tried to kidnap me. Thankfully, some bystanders recognized I was in trouble and helped. He was arrested but later killed himself in jail.

"I know," Alyssa murmurs. "That don't seem fair."

Her cell phone rings. She answers on the second ring. "Hey, boo."

I pretend to gag.

"Don't hate," Alyssa tells me.

"I got a man—I'm not hatin' on nobody."

I pick up the television remote and surf channels while Alyssa is on the phone with Stephen.

My cell phone rings.

"Dee, I'm so glad you answered your phone. I really need to talk to you."

"What's up, Mimi?"

"You won't believe what's been going on. My father's having an affair."

"No way. Have you been reading the tabloids again? You know half of that stuff isn't true."

"*It is true, Dee.* Mother found out. She wanted to surprise him in Paris. She was the one who was surprised. Father was there with his lover. She caught them in bed, Dee."

"Oh, Mimi . . . I'm so sorry."

"Mother is asking for a divorce. I can't believe this is happening to me. My life is going to change."

"You'll still have both your parents, Mimi."

"It won't be the same. You of all people know that. Look how much your life has changed."

"My life actually changed for the better." I steal a peek at Alyssa and smile. "I have a real family now."

"You can't really believe that."

"Yeah. I do."

"This can't be happening to me," Mimi moans. "I love my life the way it is—I don't want it to change."

"Mimi, your dad was hardly home. It's not like you saw him every day."

"Mother wants to move back to London. She doesn't want to stay here anymore."

"Maybe she just wants to be close to her family. It's understandable. Her heart has just been broken."

Alyssa interrupts her conversation with Stephen to ask, "What's going on with Mimi? Are her parents getting divorced?"

I nod and gesture for her to keep quiet. I don't want Mimi getting more upset. I tell her, "You never know. Your parents could work everything out."

"I'm mad at Father, too, but I think he deserves one more chance. I mean, he's never cheated on her before. At least not that we know about."

Mimi whines for the next half hour, still complaining about how much she'll have to give up if they move to London. By the time the conversation ends, I realize that Mimi is most worried about leaving her boyfriend behind.

MOM IS DOWNSTAIRS in the media room watching a movie with Aunt Phoebe, Uncle Reed, and Kevin. Alyssa wanted to join them but I refused. I don't want to be anywhere close to him. She relents and agrees to watch a movie in my bedroom.

After changing into pajamas, Alyssa and I decide which movie we're going to watch, but before I can start it, Mom knocks on the door of my bedroom, then walks inside. I can tell from her expression that she's in Mom mode and about to fuss about something.

"Mom . . . ," I begin. "Did I forget to do something?"

She stands in front of the flat-panel television, blocking my view.

"I couldn't help but notice how your attitude changed when Kevin arrived," Mom states. "He brought you a beautiful gift and even offered to buy some of your jewelry just to support you, and you try to take advantage of the situation. That's being ungrateful and downright rude. Divine, I really think you owe him an apology. Kevin has done everything in his power to get to know you a little better, and you treat him like dirt."

I don't see where I did anything wrong. I have the right to charge any price I want for my creations. "You want me to go downstairs right now and tell Kevin I'm sorry? *I'm in my pajamas.*"

"You can put on your robe."

"How about I just apologize through the intercom?" I can tell by the look on Mom's face that I'm pushing her buttons. She's getting on my nerves, too. "There's no reason for me to go downstairs half-dressed."

Mom shakes her head in disbelief.

"I'll apologize tomorrow morning. I'm sure he'll be around here then."

I thought Mom was about to slap me silly. Placing her hands on her hips, she demands, "What are you trying to say? You think he's sleeping here?"

Shrugging, I say, "I don't know what Kevin does."

"I'm tired of having this discussion with you, Divine. Kevin and I are not lovers. He's never spent the night over here. He has his own place here in Atlanta."

"He moved here to be near you though."

Mom's eyes narrow as she asks, "And you have a problem with that why?"

"Sounds like he's looking for more than friendship to me."

"I'm not going round and round with you on this. Divine, throw on a pair of jeans and a shirt—I want you to apologize to him tonight. I mean it. You owe Kevin that much."

I climb out of bed and do as I'm told.

Kevin is just about to walk out the front door when Mom calls him back inside. She pushes me toward him.

Clearing my throat, I say, "First off, I want to say I don't see where I was rude to you, but my mom seems to think I should apologize, so here goes—I'm so sorry and it won't happen again."

"Divine . . ."

I don't miss the warning tone of her voice. I'm really pushing the envelope here. Glancing over my shoulder at her, I say, "Well, you did tell me that I have to apologize to him. I did what you told me to do."

"Girl, you tapping on my last nerve. You better watch yourself."

I continue pleading my innocence. "What did I do?"

Kevin breaks into a smile. "It's fine. Divine, I accept your apology. I understand you're very protective of your mother, and I don't blame you. I'd be the same way."

"Thank you for the gift. It's very nice." I reach into my pocket and pull out four bracelets. "You can give these to your nieces. I don't have any gift boxes for them. Sorry."

"Let me pay you for them."

"Kevin, I don't want you to do that. It's my gift to you. Like Mom said, you were very generous." Stealing a peek over at Mom, I add, "Thank you for looking out for my mom."

"You're quite welcome. Have a safe trip back to Temple. I won't see you tomorrow."

I can't be totally sure, but I think Kevin seems a little too happy about that. He's already looking forward to having my mom to himself.

I can't stand Kevin Nash.

MOM COMES INTO my room the next morning while I'm getting dressed and sits down on my bed. She doesn't say much at first.

"Are you still mad at me?" I ask.

"Honey, I'm not mad at you. I'm just sitting here remembering the day you were born and how fast you grew up. It seems like yesterday that I was holding you in my arms. Now standing before me is this—"

"Fierce-looking fashion diva," I finish for her.

"Who's very humble," she adds with a laugh. "I don't know what I'm gonna do with you, baby girl."

"You could let me do whatever I want?"

"Not a chance." Mom stands up, then walks over to me with her arms outstretched.

We hug.

"I love you so much, baby girl. I miss you so much when we're apart."

"I feel the same way. I'm so glad that you're here in Atlanta. I like that I can be closer to you than when you were in California."

I steal a peek over at the clock on the bedside table and say, "I'd better hurry up and finish getting dressed."

A few minutes later, we walk downstairs to join everyone in the kitchen for one of Miss Eula's country breakfasts. The woman had to be up at the crack of dawn to prepare the feast I see spread out on the dining room table.

Uncle Reed says grace. I don't think I've ever met anyone who loves to pray as much as my uncle. He prays over everything.

Since we're leaving right after we finish eating, I can't sit and take my time to savor the food like I would normally. Uncle Reed is reminding us every five minutes that we have to hurry so that we can make it to church.

I eat as quickly as I can without choking, then finish up my cranberry juice. I have a few seconds to run back to my room and brush my teeth a second time. I can't be walking around with food stuck between them.

Uncle Reed gets on the intercom saying, "The bus is leaving. The bus is leaving."

I'm so not amused.

I meet Alyssa in the hallway. We descend the staircase together. Aunt Phoebe is already at the front door with her luggage. The Jimmy Choos I talked Mom into letting me borrow are already hurting my feet. They're fierce and I pray I'll be able to at least wear them through the service. But as soon as I get into the van, these babies are coming off.

chapter 4

We drive back to Temple. Uncle Reed likes to be at church at least a half hour before Sunday school is supposed to start at nine forty-five. The only thing to keep my uncle away from church is his getting sick. Even if he's not preaching, he's still going to be in the pulpit.

I stayed up until midnight watching the movie and then talking to Madison on my cell phone, so I'm still feeling sleepy. I hope Uncle Reed's sermon isn't boring. If it is, I'll be knocked out in the second row of the choir.

I really need my beauty sleep. I'm not staying up until one thirty tonight. The last thing I need is puffy eyes. I'm way too cute to be looking raggedy. That's for losers.

"You must have stayed up late," Uncle Reed says to me. "You slept the whole way here."

I don't respond because I'm not particularly fond of lying on church property or on Sunday. Basically, I try hard not to lie at all. I don't have to say a word because the expression on Uncle Reed's face tells me that he has a pretty good idea why I'm so tired.

Alyssa's sitting across from me with a big grin on her face. She knows I was on the phone with Madison just like I'm pretty sure she was talking to Stephen long past phone curfew. We sneak and do it all the time.

I wonder if God considers that a form of lying. One day, I'll have to ask Uncle Reed, but without telling on myself.

We climb out of the car. Alyssa follows Aunt Phoebe while I go with Uncle Reed to his office.

I wasn't about to tell him that I was on the phone late with Madison. Been there, done that, and I'd be in a load of trouble. "I wasn't up that late," I say.

"Try to stay awake during service."

I pretend to be offended by his words. "Uncle Reed, what are you trying to say? I don't fall asleep on your sermons. They are always so interesting and enlightening."

He laughs. "Really? So what did you learn from my sermon on last Sunday?"

I search my memory. What *did* he talk about?

"Just what I thought," he says, taking a seat behind his desk.

"I *do* know," I insist. "You were talking about David. You said that he was a man after God's own heart and you gave us a list of the qualities that he possessed—something like that anyway." I sit down on one of the visitor chairs.

"I guess you were listening. I'm glad to hear it."

"*I listen to you.* I don't know why you'd think I don't."

"I'm just checking. I might do that from time to time."

Folding my arms across my chest, I ask, "Uncle Reed, do you have to spot-check everything?"

He roars with laughter. "That's what being a parent is all about. I intend to know as much of your business as possible—that is, until you're old enough to handle your own interests. That includes making sure you are equipped to survive in the world."

I don't have a clue how giving me pop quizzes on his sermons helps me in the future, but okay.

> **HollywoodQT:** where have u been? I've been IMing u but didn't get a response from u.
> **SexyRhyann:** Haven't been online. My brother must b using my IM. Auntie Mom been tripping hard because I made a D n history. Like I'm gonna need 2 know about a bunch of dead people to make it n life.

I'm totally shocked. Rhyann hasn't ever made less than a B. This is so not her. Her aunt Selma is really strict. Rhyann calls her Auntie Mom because she acts just like a real mother would. At one point a few months ago she was calling her Moms, but her brothers and sisters got upset about it so she stopped. I type in my response.

> **HollywoodQT:** What's up with the D? Ur 2 smart 2 b making D's.
> **SexyRhyann:** History is boring. I have 2 many papers 2 write and it's messing up my life. Carson and I don't have much time 2 spend 2gether as it is. I need time with my man.
> **HollywoodQT:** But if u don't keep your grades up, ur not going 2 b able 2 see him at all. U know how parents trip on stuff like that.
> **SexyRhyann:** Tru. I'm supposed 2 b online right

now doing research for a history paper due on
Monday.
HollywoodQT: Get back 2 work then. I'll call you
tomorrow. I just got back from Atlanta this morn-
ing and I need to get my clothes ready for school.
The weekends go by way 2 fast.
SexyRhyann: Tru. Talk 2 u l8tr. Better get back 2
work on this stupid project.

I sign off and shut down my computer. Rhyann has gone completely nuts over her latest boyfriend. She's never been one to mess
around on her studies, so she must really like this Carson guy.

I'm crazy about Madison and I want to spend all of my time
with him, so I totally understand where she's coming from. And
she's right—who really needs history? It's not like we're going to
need it to get a job. Unless you're a history teacher.

I spend the next hour working on my latest hobby—designing
bracelets. I pick which beads will be used for the one I'm working
on now.

Aunt Phoebe found these purple ones with specks of gold that
I really like, so I lay them out on my desk, placing tiny gold beads
between them to use as spacers. After choosing some lavender ones
to break up the color, I cut the thread and knot it at the ends.

I can hear Alyssa singing in the hallway. A few minutes later,
she enters my bedroom.

"What are you doing?"

"I'm making a bracelet. What does it look like I'm doing?" My
cousin can be a little slow at times but I love her.

"Ooh, I like that one. Can I have one like that?"

"If you pay me, you can have whatever you want."

"You're gonna actually make me pay for a bracelet?" she huffs.
"You gave me three of them already."

"That's exactly why you should pay me for this one. It's like one of those book clubs in the magazines. You get three free, but you have to pay full price for the fourth one."

"You're rich, remember? You don't need the money."

"That's beside the point. It costs money to make these bracelets. I need to recoup my investment."

"I'll remember that the next time you want me to *give* you a pair of earrings or one of my necklaces."

"Let me see what you have, and if there's something I like, we can make a trade. How about that?"

Alyssa sits down on the edge of my bed. "Guess what?"

I turn around. "What?"

"Stephen asked me to . . . you know."

"Have sex?"

She nods, prompting me to ask, "What did you say?"

"I didn't really tell him anything. I didn't know what to say."

"What do you mean you didn't know what to say?" I demand. "*No* works real good." I notice she's staring at something on the floor. Only there's nothing there.

"You're lying," I say. "I can tell when you're not telling the truth."

I get up and close the door to my bedroom. "Alyssa, you can't be thinking about giving up your virginity. You see the mess your brother's in. He's about to be a daddy in a few short weeks. And I know you remember how Aunt Phoebe was when she found out. She had a hissy fit."

"I love him, Divine. But I didn't say I was gonna do it. I just didn't tell Stephen no. I was scared to because of the way Madison treated you when you told him that you wanted to wait."

"If Stephen really cares for you, he'll wait."

"You're right. I'm scared of losing him but I'm scared of Mama more."

"Aunt Phoebe is scary. Seriously though, we need to try and hold out as long as we can. There's too much stuff out there in the world . . . diseases you can't get rid of and pregnancy."

"On top of that, it's a sin. I know all that, but it doesn't change the way I feel whenever I'm around Stephen." Letting out a long sigh, Alyssa says, "Trying to be a Christian is so hard at times."

"Just think of what your mom will do to you if she ever finds out—works for me every time."

MIA AND I meet after our fourth-period class to walk down to the cafeteria together. We're meeting Alyssa and Penny there for lunch.

"I haven't seen Stacy at all today." Stacy and I have English together and I let her borrow my notes. Now I need them back. I need to brush up before our test tomorrow. "Do you know if she came to school?"

Mia shrugs. "I haven't seen her either. She wasn't in first period." She pulls out her wallet from her backpack. "Did you and Alyssa have fun in Atlanta? I wish I could've gone with y'all. I know you had a good time."

We find an empty table and quickly snag it. I'm so glad we got here early enough to grab one. The cafeteria gets crowded pretty quickly.

"We had a good time," I respond. "You should've come with us. Miss Eula and Mom both asked about you."

Mia's eyes drop down to her hands. "I really wanted to go, but Tim—he was coming over to the house."

"You could've called and told him that you were going to Atlanta with us. I know you're not going to just sit around waiting for him to come by. Right?"

"It wasn't like that. We'd made plans to hang out before you told me y'all were going. Tim's real jealous. He would've thought I was trying to go see some dude."

"So, what do your parents think about him?"

"They like him."

I'm like totally surprised. *"They do?"*

She nods. "They're not crazy in love with him, but as long as he treats me fine, they don't have a problem with Tim."

"Mia, I have to be honest with you. I don't think Tim treats you that well. He just doesn't seem that nice to me."

"It's just that you don't really know him, Divine. He's a nice guy."

"He seems like he has a real quick temper. I always hear that he's about to fight someone at school. Tim stays in the principal's office."

"Tim does have a temper," Mia admits. "But it's not always his fault. You know how people get at school when there's a new person—they try you. It doesn't mean anything."

"A lot of people are scared of him."

Mia chuckles. "That's because he don't take no mess off nobody. They try him and get beat down. If Tim cares about you, he's a sweetheart and he's very protective. I'm not trying to make him out to be perfect, but he's not a bad person either."

"Then why do you look so scared whenever he's around?"

"I don't . . . I'm not scared of Tim."

I wasn't convinced. "Mia, you're my girl and all . . . you don't have to lie to me. I have two very good eyes and I can see what's happening. I know you have feelings for this guy, but you need to be careful. Tim has an attitude and with a quick temper—it's a bad combination."

"Divine, what are people telling you?"

"About what?"

"Me and Tim. Where are you coming up with all this?"

"I saw him at the dance, Mia. I've seen the way he treats you at school. Nobody needs to tell me anything."

She doesn't respond.

Alyssa and Penny take that moment to show up.

"It's about time," I tell them. "I was about to get my food and just forget about you two."

"I had to talk to my boo," Penny tells me. "He's not feeling well and is about to leave school. I'm not gonna see him the rest of the day."

"You'll live," I respond. "But I might not if I don't eat something soon."

While Alyssa and Penny put down their backpacks, I rise to my feet, saying, "C'mon, Mia. Let's get in line."

While we're waiting for our turn to choose our lunch selections, I notice that she keeps rubbing her right arm. "Did you hurt your arm?"

"I hit it on a door."

Alyssa and Penny join us.

"When we were on our way here, I saw Mr. McPhearson talking to Tim," Penny announces. "I don't know what was going on, but your boyfriend didn't look too happy."

If the principal was talking to him, it can't be good, I think to myself.

"He just doesn't like Tim," Mia says. "Mr. McPhearson's been giving him a hard time from the first day he walked into the school."

"Tim's done his share of dirt," I say. "Remember he jumped on Tommy Jones. Just because the boy accidentally stepped on his foot."

"It was more than that," Mia states. "Divine, you don't know the whole story."

"Why don't you tell us?" Penny says. "Tommy doesn't bother nobody. He's quiet and very shy. Tim didn't have to beat him up like that."

"He got smart with Tim."

"Your boyfriend shouldn't be so sensitive," I say.

"None of us were there so we shouldn't be making assumptions." Mia picks up a tray and a couple of napkins. "Tim just don't take no mess off nobody. He ain't no punk. People just need to stay out his face."

"Why you being so defensive?" I inquire.

"I'm not."

We carry our food-laden trays over to our table and settle around it to eat lunch.

We overheard a couple of boys talking about Tim at the next table.

"I wish people would just shut up sometimes," Mia mutters. Standing up, she blurts, "I forgot that I needed to go to the library. I need to get a book for a research paper I have to do in history class."

"Want me to go with you?"

"If you want to."

"Mia, I didn't mean to make you mad—it's just you're my friend and I care about you."

"I'm glad you care about me, but, Divine . . . you need to trust me. Things are so good between me and Tim. He's a good guy. The only reason he got mad at the dance was because he thought I was dissing him."

"Why'd he think that?"

"I was paying more attention to you and Alyssa than him. I'm sure Madison and Stephen probably felt the same way."

"Naaw," I respond. "We didn't do anything but go to the bathroom. They don't trip over stuff like that."

"We were in there for a while."

"Maybe ten minutes," I countered.

"Tim thought we were gone too long."

"The boy can't be away from you more than a minute. What's his problem?"

"He loves me," Mia states with a smile. "My last boyfriend kept complaining because I wanted to be around him all the time. Tim enjoys my company."

"But he shouldn't be getting mad because you're hanging with your friends—that's so not cool."

"Divine, it wasn't like that."

"Then how was it, Mia? We were gone a few minutes and your boy started tripping when we got back to the table."

"I've already told you. Look, let's just change the subject, because we're getting nowhere. I know Tim a whole lot better than you do."

"I don't know him at all, but I *do* know what I see."

Mia sighs loudly.

"Fine, I'll drop it for now. I just don't want to see you get hurt. That's all I'm saying."

"You don't have anything to worry about, Divine."

"If you say so."

After our little conversation, Mia avoids me for the rest of the day. I leave a message on her cell phone later that evening, but she doesn't call me back.

I guess she's pretty mad at me right now. I don't really care. I haven't said anything to hurt Mia. I take my BF responsibility seriously and I'm committed to making sure she doesn't end up with some whack job for a boyfriend.

Mia's so desperate for a boyfriend sometimes. She thinks that it looks bad when a girl is alone. I mean, some girls do look lame when they can't catch a man, but there is a way to play it off. You just have to walk around looking fierce all the time.

Until Mia met Tim, she was walking around school wearing Levi's jeans and Hanes T-shirts or some tacky-looking sweatshirt. She dresses a little better, not much, but there's a definite improvement since they started going together.

Alyssa and I have a Y-Club meeting after school. She's already in the classroom by the time I get there.

"Hey, what's up with Mia?" Alyssa inquires. "She was acting kind of funny today."

"She's got some stuff going on."

"She got very defensive whenever we mentioned Tim. I thought maybe she got mad or something. We weren't trying to talk about him—everything we said was the truth."

"If Mia was upset, she'll get over it. Truth is truth. You can't be so sensitive when you're dating a jerk."

"Well, I hope she's not mad."

I dismiss Alyssa's concerns with a wave of my hand. "Don't worry about Mia. Believe me, she'll be all right."

Our adviser opens the meeting with a prayer. The Y-Club is the only Christian club in school. Chance and Alyssa had to talk me into joining. I didn't think I'd like being a member, but it's not as bad as I thought it would be.

We turn in our registration for the upcoming Christian Life Conference in April. Alyssa and I are looking forward to going. Chance went last year and came home talking about how much he enjoyed it. The CLC is when Y-Club members get together to fellowship through workshops, drama, speakers, music, and games with each other.

After the meeting, Chance has to stop by Trina's house, so Alyssa and I walk in the other direction, heading home.

"Did you talk to Stephen?"

Alyssa nods. "We didn't get a chance to talk long because I had to come to the meeting, but I told him the truth. He wasn't too happy, Divine." Her eyes fill with tears. "I think he's gonna break up with me."

"Madison broke up with me, but you see he came running back. Stephen loves you, Alyssa. He'll understand."

"I hope so. I don't want to lose him."

"You won't. At least I don't think you will. Stephen really does love you."

"Madison loved you but he still broke up with you," Alyssa points out.

"And he's working overtime to get me back. The brotha realizes what he was losing."

"I don't want to go through that, Divine."

"I don't want that for you either. Look, Alyssa, if Stephen leaves you over this, then maybe you're not supposed to be together. I know you don't want to think about that, but it is a possibility."

"You're right."

I hate seeing Alyssa look so sad. I silently vow to beat Stephen with Aunt Phoebe's bat if he breaks my cousin's heart.

Her cell phone rings.

"It's Stephen," she announces. "I don't know what to do. Should I talk to him or let it go to voice mail?"

"I think you should go on and talk to him."

I try hard not to pay attention to their conversation, but it's not easy. Alyssa tries explaining her feelings to him. I hate that I can't hear his responses. Silently, I pray for God to make Stephen understand. I don't want to see my cousin get her heart broken.

Alyssa's doing this for Him, after all.

chapter 5

When the three-twenty bell rings the next day, I have to re-strain myself to keep from jumping up with glee. I'm too happy to be getting out of school. This has been a trying day for me.

First, I couldn't find my history homework, and Mrs. Whit-comb had the nerve to treat me as if I were lying about it. I'm on the honor roll and I make good grades. Why would I have to lie about something as simple as homework? Even when I don't feel like doing it, I get it done.

Then that stupid big mouth, Mae, accuses me of talking to the nasty dog she calls a boyfriend. She's never liked me from the moment I strolled into Temple High School. As if I'd want anything to do with Cedric. He's after anything with boobs and a skirt. Like I'd relish being a notch on his bedpost.

I'm so looking forward to going home and just forgetting about this day. I make a brief stop at my locker before leaving the building to meet Alyssa and Nicholas. Stephen sometimes walks with us, but lately he's been tutoring a couple of students.

"Where's Nicholas?" Alyssa questions when she walks up to me after school.

Shrugging, I say, "I don't know. I thought he'd be waiting on us by now. He's usually the first one standing here by the fence."

I hear my name being called and turn around to find Madison, with his good-looking self, coming toward us. "Here comes my boo."

Alyssa chuckles. "Thought you two weren't back together."

"We're not. But he's still my boo."

Wearing a big grin on his face, Madison says, "Hey, Divine, you sure looking good today."

I fold my arms across my chest and ask, "Are you saying I don't look good any other day?"

He laughs. "You know what I mean." His eyes travel from my head to my toes, then back up. "You are so fine."

I smile. "What are you up to?"

"Looking for you. I haven't seen you all day. I thought for a minute that you were absent until I ran into Chance. He told me that you came to school."

"I've been right here all day. Your attentions must have been elsewhere. I guess you looking around for a girlfriend."

He shakes his head in denial. "I don't need to look—I got one. *You.*"

"Naaah. We're not together. Remember?"

"As far as I'm concerned, it's only a matter of time. You and I will never be just friends. There's too much emotion between us."

I laugh. "Whatever . . ."

"You know we belong together, Divine. Just admit it."

"Madison, we've talked about this before. I'm not rushing back to you. You have to give me some space."

I steal a glance over my shoulder to where Alyssa's standing and trying her hardest to hear what we're saying. I know she's trying to listen. Why, I don't know. I'll tell her everything later anyway.

Madison grabs my hand. "Divine, please give me another chance. I'm crazy about you. Tomorrow's Valentine's Day. I bought somethin' nice for you but you can't have it unless you're my girl."

"I know you're not trying to blackmail me."

"It's not like that, Divine. I'm just saying it's a girlfriend kind of gift. That's all."

"I still have feelings for you, Madison. I just need to take some time and really think about us. Just give me a few days. Okay?"

His smile disappears. "I guess I don't have a choice."

Stephen strolls over to Alyssa, saying, "I don't have to tutor anybody today." Alyssa starts grinning from ear to ear. He wraps an arm around her and they start walking home.

Madison and I follow a short distant away so that we can continue our conversation.

"I hope you're not mad at me," I say to Madison. "All I'm asking for is a few more days. It's not like you're going anywhere. We still talk all the time, so why are you tripping?"

"I don't want to lose you, Divine. All these dudes around here trying to be with you. I kinda wanted us to get back together for Valentine's."

"Madison, I don't want any of them. And it's not like I haven't noticed the girls in your face. I'm not sleeping—I see them. As for Valentine's . . . that's so sweet."

"I want you back."

His words bring a smile to my face.

"You don't mind me walking you home, do you?"

I shake my head no. "That's fine."

"So what's going on between you and Nicholas?"

His question stops me in my tracks. "What are you talking about?"

"I see he's been walking you home lately. And I see y'all talking all the time at school. I heard that he wants to go with you."

I laugh. "Nicholas and I walk home together because he lives on the way to my uncle's house. We also have a tae kwon do class together. Most of all, he is my friend. Madison, he and I are just friends. *That's all.*"

"Has he asked you to go with him?"

"No," I reply. "Madison, I can't believe you acting all jealous. I went to the dance with you. Remember? Nicholas took somebody else."

"Did he ask you to go?"

I shake my head and laugh. "No. Nicholas never considered asking me as far as I know."

"I'm tripping, huh?"

"Big-time. Madison, I'll have an answer for you tomorrow. How about that?"

"Only if it's the right answer. I don't want no bad news on Valentine's Day."

I switch my backpack from one side to the other. "I wouldn't do that to anybody."

"I love you, girl. I mean that."

Madison's declaration makes me feel all tingly inside. I'm crazy about my boo, but there's that tiny part of me that's afraid to take him back. I don't want to be hurt again—especially by the same boy. I try not to make the same mistake twice when it comes to stuff like this.

Stephen and Madison walk with us until we get to their street.

"I hope you'll think about what I said," Madison tells me. He gives me a quick hug and kiss before he and Stephen leave us.

I'm surprised to see Nicholas already home when we near his house. What did he do? Run all the way home?

"Hey, y'all," he greets.

"Where werc you after school?" I ask. "Alyssa and I waited for you by the fence."

Alyssa says, "I'ma go on home. I need to get my homework out of the way so that I can make some stuff for Aunt Shirley. She wants to show them to the ladies in her book club. Divine, she wants you to make some bracelets to match."

"Okay," I respond. I turn my attention back to Nicholas. "So what happened to you?"

Pushing his glasses upward, he responds, "I saw you talking to Madison and I didn't want to interrupt."

"You wouldn't have interrupted anything, Nicholas. We were just talking."

He shrugged. "You two looked pretty intense."

"He wants us to get back together. Madison's been asking me for weeks now but I needed some time to think."

"So what are you gonna do?"

Shrugging, I respond, "I don't know. What do you think I should do?"

"Take it slow. You don't want Madison to think you're just gonna run back to him."

"Do you think he really cares about me?"

"I guess. Madison and I been in school together since we were in kindergarten, but I don't know him in the way you do. Know what I mean?"

I nod in understanding. "He cares for me. I'm sure of it."

"And you still have feelings for him. He's all you talk about— you might as well go back to him."

"Thanks . . . I think."

Nicholas walks through the gate, closing it behind him. "C'mon, I'll walk you the rest of the way home."

"I can't believe you bailed out on me and Alyssa like that because of Madison. We're friends, Nicholas. You don't have to do that."

He shrugs in nonchalance. "Hey, I was just trying to give you and your boyfriend some space."

"He's not my boyfriend yet."

"He will be. Madison is the only boy you ever talk about. I'm surprise you've held out this long. Just go on and take him back. It's what you really want to do."

"What about you? Why don't you have a girlfriend? There are some nice girls at Temple High."

"I'm doing my thing."

"Uh-huh . . . If you say so—you better stop being so quiet and shy."

He laughs. "Divine, you don't have to worry about me. I have everything under control."

"Is that your polite way of telling me to mind my own business?"

"Just telling you that I'm good."

We reach the house just as Uncle Reed is pulling into the driveway. Nicholas waves at him, then tells me, "I'll see you later. I better get back so I can get started on my science project."

Nicholas stops walking when we reach the mailbox.

"Thanks for walking me home. See you tomorrow."

"Give Madison a second chance," he urges before dashing off down the street.

Uncle Reed waits for me on the porch. "That's a nice young man," he says.

"Nicholas and I are just friends," I clarify. "He's more like a brother to me."

"I was simply making an observation—not trying to matchmake."

I gaze at Uncle Reed to see if he's serious.

He winks. "It's always good to explore all of your options. Although right now your focus should be on what college you're planning on attending and studying for the SAT you'll be taking in a couple of weeks."

"You really know how to ruin a good mood, Uncle Reed."

"Just trying to help you stay focused."

"Don't you think you've done enough? Aren't you getting bored with telling me the same thing over and over again? Believe it or not, I heard you the first time."

Uncle Reed wrapped an arm around me. "I'll never get tired of looking out for the people I care about."

"You're way too dedicated," I mutter.

Inside the house, I spend a few minutes with Aunt Phoebe before heading to my room to study. If my aunt and uncle weren't home, I'd be doing whatever instead of homework. But since they're here in the house, I study to avoid any chores that Aunt Phoebe loves to surprise us with. Last week, she had me and Alyssa clean out the garage. I don't recall ever seeing so many spiders and crazy-looking bugs in my life. I'm not putting myself in that position again.

IT'S MY TURN to wash dishes, and after trying to talk Alyssa into trading with me and failing, I resign myself that I'm doomed to have dishpan hands.

Aunt Phoebe forgot to pick up some rubber gloves. A part of me wonders if she did it on purpose. She's always giving me a hard time about wearing them in the first place.

I look down at the sink of soapy water, thinking, *This totally sucks*.

"My hands are going to be so wrinkly," I complain when Alyssa strolls into the kitchen.

"That's okay," she assures me with a laugh. "You can always buy some new ones since you're so rich. What's that so many people are doing now? Getting Botox. Maybe you can get Botox injections for your hands."

Using the sponge, I wash all of the glasses first, then start on the plates. "I read that if you have sweaty palms, the Botox injections might help. I don't have sweaty anything—I'm not one of those people who sweat. I perspire."

"You not only sweat, Divine, but you stink, too."

I wave off her words. I don't know who Alyssa is referring to—I'm not a woman who smells.

Not me. No way.

Handing her a plastic container I've just washed and rinsed, I say, "Girl, don't be hatin' over there. I'm not like you, cuz. I didn't have to grow up on the farm. My body isn't built like yours."

"Give it up, Divine. I'm sorry to bust your Hollywood bubble, but you're still one of us. You're still a GRITS."

"A *grit*? You're comparing me to a grit?" I'm like so totally insulted. Alyssa's about to fall down a few notches on the BFF chain. She just dissed me.

"G-R-I-T-S . . . it's an acronym for 'girls raised in the South.' Haven't you heard that before?"

I shake my head no. "Sorry. I don't keep up with cute little Southern sayings. I just like the boys."

"*One* boy, you mean."

"Okay . . . I'm crazy about Madison. But I'm also a little insecure when it comes to him. I'd never in a million years tell him that. I'm not about to let him break my heart a second time.

"Alyssa, tell me the truth," I begin. "Do you honestly think I should take Madison back? You know that's why he wanted to talk to me after school, don't you?"

"Yeah. I thought so. Madison's a real nice guy. But I wouldn't do it right away. I think I'd make him wait a little longer."

"That's what Nicholas told me."

"He's a boy. I guess he should know."

I agree.

Lowering her voice to a whisper, she tells me, "Madison really loves you, Divine. Stephen says you're all the boy talks about. You just need to let him know that you have other options."

"What options?"

"Any other options. Divine, there are boys trying to get with you all the time. Madison sees this because he's always fussing about it to Stephen."

I laugh. "He's so jealous."

"Yeah. Girl, he was ready to fight some boy in his science class because he was talking about getting with you."

"Really?" I study Alyssa's face to make sure she's not teasing me.

"Uh-huh."

"I got Madison a card for tomorrow. I didn't buy him a present because we weren't together. Now I feel bad. He got me one."

Alyssa shrugs. "He should understand. You two weren't together."

"I'm going to take Madison back. I'll tell him tomorrow and that'll be my gift to him."

"Works for me," Alyssa responds. "Stephen bought me something, too. I bought him some cologne."

"That's nice," I murmur. "He'll like that."

"Madison's gon' be real happy when he finds out you two are getting back together."

"He'd better be. This is his last chance with me, so I hope and pray he'll treat me right. But if he doesn't, that'll be the end of us for good. *I mean that.*"

"I don't think you have anything to worry about, Divine. Madison's worked too hard to get you back."

"I hope you're right. I don't need no drama. I've had enough to last me a lifetime. Speaking of drama . . . I need to write my dad back before I go to bed tonight. All he can see to talk about is Ava and the baby she's carrying. I think he's more excited about their child than he ever was with me."

"Are you feeling jealous?" Alyssa inquires.

"No. No way. Why should I be jealous? In a few years I'll be in college and on my own."

"I think it's normal for you to feel that way—if you do."

"I don't. I'm totally fine." I'm not feeling this conversation so I change the subject. "I saw Trina up at school today. She looks like she's gotten even bigger. I didn't think it was possible."

"I talked to her last night. She didn't tell me she was coming up to the school."

"I didn't talk to her because I didn't want to be late for class. She was in the office with her mom."

I stretch and yawn. "I'm so tired, but I still need to finish my homework."

"I need to finish up my math. I hate trig."

I frown. "I don't even want to think about it. Not tonight. I have enough to do."

We go our separate ways. Alyssa in her room and me in mine.

Half an hour later, my homework is finished and I let out a sigh of relief. I'm distracted by my thoughts of Madison and how I believe he's going to react when I tell him that we're getting back together.

After a quick shower, I walk into my closet to select clothes for tomorrow. Since it's going to be Valentine's Day, I pick out a pair of red leather pants and a red-and-white-striped sweater. I wrap my hair and tie it up because I want to wear it down tomorrow.

I'm going to look so fierce.

Madison calls me just as I settle into bed. We don't talk long because Aunt Phoebe comes to my room to talk about some church function she wants me and Alyssa to sing at. Aunt Phoebe's pimping us. She's always volunteering our voices. She says we should be using our talents for the Lord.

I need all the points I can get for heaven. Plus I think I want to sing in the heavenly choir, so I need God to hear me every chance I get. I guess I'm auditioning.

When Aunt Phoebe leaves, I check the clock. It's almost eleven o'clock. Too late to call Madison back. I'm okay with it though—I don't want to slip up and tell him what I've planned for his present. I want to officially get back with him tomorrow.

I can hardly wait to see his face.

chapter 6

I can't wait to get to school. I rush Alyssa and Chance through breakfast, hoping to get there early enough to talk to Madison before the bell rings.

He calls me at seven forty-five and asks me, "What time you leaving the house?"

"In a few minutes. I'm ready but I have to wait on Alyssa and Chance. Why?"

"I'ma meet y'all on the corner. Tell Alyssa that Stephen's gonna be there, too."

"See you then." I go to Alyssa and whisper, "Madison's going to meet me at the corner. Hurry up."

Aunt Phoebe strolls out of her bedroom with a head full of pink curlers, a tropical-print muumuu, and bedroom slippers. I'm surprised because she's usually dressed by now.

"Happy Valentine's Day," I say while giving her the card I bought her. Upon closer inspection, I can see that Aunt Phoebe's eyes are puffy and her nose is red. "You don't look like you're feeling too well."

"I'm coming down with something. I'm getting ready to make me some tea."

"I hope you feel better."

"Me, too, sugar."

Alyssa joins us. She hands Aunt Phoebe a handmade card. "Happy Valentine's Day." While she's inquiring about her mom's health, Chance comes up and does the same—hands Aunt Phoebe a greeting card.

We have cards for Uncle Reed, too, but this is his prayer time so we know not to disturb him in his office. We leave his cards on the kitchen table on top of his newspaper.

Madison and Stephen are standing on the corner.

"Y'all knew they was gonna be here?" Chance questions.

"Yeah," we say in unison.

Stephen takes Alyssa by the hand. "Happy Valentine's Day."

Madison embraces me and whispers, "I hope you have some good news for me."

I meet his gaze. "Madison, I want to be with you."

"For real?" he asks as if I'd kid about something like that.

"I don't play when it comes to my emotions or anybody else's. You should know that about me already."

Chance clears his throat. "We need to keep moving. I don't want to be late for my first-period class. Y'all can talk while we walk."

We arrive on campus ten minutes before the bell rings. Madison and I sit down on a bench, discussing our relationship. He hands me a present.

I tear into it.

"Madison . . . oh my goodness! This is so beautiful." My eyes tear up. Madison had taken the picture we took at the Sweethearts' Dance and had it placed on a charm.

"I know you love that charm bracelet you wear, so I thought this would be a nice addition."

I hug him. "Thank you so much, Madison. I love this."

I reach into my backpack and retrieve the card I bought for him. "I didn't buy you a present. We weren't together at the time and—"

"Getting you back is gift enough for me," Madison responds before I can finish.

That's why he's my boo.

The bell rings and we have to part. Madison kisses me on the lips before rushing off to his class located on the other end of the campus.

I spend my time in the first two classes daydreaming about him.

"You look horrible," I tell Mia when I run into her outside the girls' locker room. We have PE together third period. "What's wrong with you?"

"I don't feel good."

"Are you coming down with something?" Taking a step backward, I add, "My aunt Phoebe is sick, too. All y'all sick people need to just stay away from me because I don't want whatever it is you might have."

Mia shrugs. "I don't think I'm coming down with a cold or anything. I just feel bad."

"What did Tim get you for Valentine's?"

"He gave me a rose."

I stare at her, waiting to hear the rest of it.

When she doesn't say anything, I ask, "Is that it? That's all he gave you? He did give you a card along with the rose at least?"

"Just the rose. It's romantic."

"But didn't you buy him a chain or something?" I'm still having trouble digesting that Tim only gave her a rose.

She nods.

"And all you got was a rose?" One rose. Talk about cheap.

"What did you get from Madison?" Mia asks. "I know you didn't buy him anything."

"We just got back together today. He says my being his girlfriend is gift enough. He didn't want anything else."

"So what did he give you?"

"A charm for my bracelet. It's a picture of me and him. The one we took at the Valentine's Dance."

Mia leans against the wall, rubbing her arm.

"Maybe you should just tell Coach McCall you're sick, so you won't have to put on your PE clothes. We're supposed to dress out today. If you don't say anything, you could get an F."

"I'ma talk to her in a minute. I just need to put my backpack away. It's killing my shoulder."

"I'll see you in a few. I need to change into my uniform." I leave Mia beside her locker.

When I walk into the gym a few minutes later, I see Mia talking to Coach McCall, our health and personal-fitness teacher. I take a seat on the bleachers along with the other students in my class.

"I don't know why she going with that thug," I hear someone say in a low whisper.

"He's fine," someone else responds.

Without turning around, I say, "Y'all really need to mind your own business."

"Shut up, Divine."

I glance over my shoulder. "I'm not the one speculating in other people's affairs."

Coach McCall and Mia walk over, putting an end to our conversation.

"I don't have to dress out," Mia whispers to me.

Before I can respond, Coach McCall orders us down on the gym floor to line up for exercise. I glance over at Mia.

She gives me a tiny smile, then rubs her arm.

I notice Mia seems to be doing that a lot.

We're playing basketball today and I'm so not in the mood. I'm not into playing sports, but since my participation counts toward my grade, I surrender. I run up and down the court trying to look like I'm really into the game, but deep down I'm begging for mercy.

Please, God . . . please let this period go by fast.

I notice Mia when she gets up and walks over to the locker room, going inside.

Five minutes pass and I begin to worry. I hope she hasn't passed out or anything. Another five minutes go by and still no Mia, so I ask Coach McCall if I can check on her.

I run off to the locker room, pushing the door wide open.

I find Mia standing in front of a full-length mirror.

"Girl, I was worried about yo—" I stop short when I see her right arm and the dark bruising. "Mia, what's wrong with your arm?"

She slips back into her sweater. "It's nothing."

"That doesn't look like nothing. I'm not stupid. Those are bruises on your arm. Tell me, what happened?"

"I took a bad fall."

Does she really expect me to believe that?

"I don't think so. Mia, tell me the truth . . . who did this to you? Did your parents do this?"

"*Girl, no.* My parents don't hit me."

"Then who did this to you?"

"Divine, drop it," Mia snaps in frustration. "I already told you what happened. I don't know why you're trying to make more of it. Don't be trying to start no rumors."

I'm offended. "Since when do I go around starting rumors? Girl, you seriously tripping. I'm outta here." I walk briskly to the exit. I don't have to take this mess off anybody. I'm only trying to help the girl.

"Divine, please wait! I'm sorry for snapping at you. It's just that I . . ."

I turn around to face her. "Mia, I thought we were friends. Excuse me for caring what happens to you."

"Divine, I'm telling you the truth. I hurt myself when I fell. That's all."

I don't believe her. "How did you fall?"

"Huh?"

"How did you fall down? The bruises on your arm look like somebody grabbed you a little too tight. They don't look like they're from a fall."

"I'm real clumsy at times."

I can feel it deep down in my stomach that Mia's lying—trying to protect someone, and if it wasn't her parents—it had to be Tim.

"Mia, I'm your friend. You can tell me anything."

My words are met with silence.

I stand there watching Mia, who looks like she torn. Finally she says, "Divine, I need you to promise me that you won't say a word to anybody about this. If I don't have your word, I'm not telling you a thing."

"I promise. Mia, I won't tell a soul."

"Not even your cousin. I know how close you and Alyssa are, but you can't talk about this to another person."

"I won't breathe a word of it, Mia. I promise."

"I lied to you earlier. You were right. I didn't fall down," she confesses. "Tim and I had a huge fight . . . an argument really. When I tried to walk away from him, he grabbed my arm a little hard. Tim didn't mean to be so rough, Divine. He was just upset."

"Mia—"

"I know what you're thinking and it's not like that. He didn't mean to hurt me. You should've seen him. Divine, he started crying and everything when he saw what he'd done. He kept saying over and over how sorry he was. I don't want you getting the wrong idea. He's a nice guy."

"Yeah," I mumble. "I can see just how nice he is."

"It's not like that."

"If you say so."

"Divine, please don't say anything about this," Mia begs. "I don't want people all up in my business and getting the wrong idea about Tim."

"You don't have to worry about me telling anyone a thing. But, Mia, I have to be honest. I think you should break up with Tim."

"Divine, it's not really your business. I don't go around here telling you about your relationship with Madison."

"He's not hitting on me."

"Tim didn't hit me either, Divine. He just grabbed my arm."

"Well, Madison doesn't grab on me enough to leave bruises. Look, Mia, I'm not trying to argue with you. I care about you and I just don't want you going out like this. *That's all*."

I walk toward the nearest exit. "We'd better get back out there. Coach McCall will be looking for us. I came in here to check on you."

"It's not a big deal, Divine. It was just an accident."

I nod. Deep down, I'm not buying any of what Mia's saying. I can't believe she believes her own words. Tim is crazy. I've been saying that from the first time I saw him.

My girl better watch out.

* * *

THE PERSON I see as soon as I leave the girls' locker room is Tim. I try to walk past him without acknowledging him, but he steps right into my path.

"Hey, you see Mia?"

"Yeah."

"Is she still in the locker room?"

"I saw her in class but I don't have any idea where she is right now," I say before stepping around him.

"Hey, your name is Divine, right?"

"Yeah."

"Can you go into the locker room for me and let Mia know that I'm out here waiting for her?"

I look at him like he's lost his last mind. "I'm not going that way. Mia will come out here when she's ready."

He says something that I'm pretty positive isn't very nice, but I'm not even listening to the jerk. Tim might have Mia scared of him, but I'm not the one.

Before I leave, I catch a glimpse of Mia rushing out, her backpack in her hand.

"Tim," she calls out. "I had to go back for my purse."

Why is she explaining anything to that jerk? I wonder.

In a way I feel bad for her because Mia's probably with him only because he's intimidated her. I shake my head sadly. I hope she finds a way out of this relationship before it gets worse.

I DON'T WANT to spill Mia's secret to anyone, but it's really bothering me. I can't tell Alyssa because she knows her. Mimi talks way too much—she could slip and say something around her mother, who will get on the phone and call mine. I can't risk that happening.

That leaves Rhyann.

Since she is the only expert I know on everything concerning boys.

"I'm glad you picked up," I tell her when she answers. "I really need to talk to you, but you have to promise me that you won't say a word to Mimi."

"Dee, you know you can trust me. What's up?"

"There's this girl I know. Her boyfriend is getting rough with her. She made me promise not to tell anyone, but I have a really bad feeling about this. I just needed to talk to someone."

"Girl, you need to tell her to dump that old boy. He sounds like he's crazy."

"I know." Finally! Someone else who sees this boy for the fool that he is. "He's trouble. I keep telling her that."

"If she's that scared of him, he's not just grabbing her arm. Divine, I bet he's also hitting on her. I have a friend of a friend who was getting beat down by her boyfriend. Girl, it was ugly. She finally was able to get away from him by going to live with her aunt in Sacramento. She had to get up outta Los Angeles. He'd threatened to kill her whole family. Even tried to set their house on fire."

"They didn't have him arrested?"

"I think so. But talk to your girl. She don't want to end up in the news."

I shake my head no. "It's not like that, Rhyann. I know she wouldn't go out like that. She wouldn't put up with no boy hitting on her. I know that for sure."

"Well, that's what it sounds like to me. You know my cousin Shirley, right?" Not waiting on a response from me, she continues, "Well, her best friend, she was in an abusive relationship. Her boyfriend had been kicking her tail since she was in the eighth grade. She moved in with him after they graduated high school and he was still beating her up. Almost killed her."

"He might be crazy, but I don't think he's insane enough to put his hands on her. Her dad's a big man and he looks like he could kill you with one hand."

"Talk to your friend, Dee. Make sure she's all right. I know how crazy it gets in the real world. You and Mimi—y'all too sheltered. You gotta walk out those mansions and stroll over here to see the real side of life. I keep telling y'all that."

I laugh. "Rhyann, you're crazy."

"I'm serious. See, I don't have to worry about that 'cause I got some crazy brothers and a family full of big, black, and mean uncles. Nobody's crazy enough to bother me. You need to see how the real world lives. Hollywood gives you a false sense of security. Girl, you better take the blinders off."

"Get off the soapbox, please," I beg. "I'm as far removed from Hollywood as anyone can get."

"But you still got that Hollywood mentality."

"Rhyann . . ."

"Okay, I'll drop it for now, but you know I'm right."

"I'd better get off the phone. We're about to have dinner and then we're playing Scrabble."

"You guys still do that?" she asks with a laugh.

"Every Thursday. We have a good time together. You and your family should do family game night."

"I don't think so. We tried Bible study one time and, girl . . . it was so much drama. My aunt Mary is Catholic; my granny is Baptist; I'm thinking about becoming Jewish; and Auntie Mom is her own special person. We don't need to do anything together—it won't work out."

I crack up. "Rhyann, you're so stupid."

"Actually, I'm pretty brilliant. I have the highest SAT scores in the school."

"No way," I say. "What happened to the D in history?"

"Girl, I had to get my head together. Carson is fine and all, but I can't be flunking no classes for him. I'm on scholarship at Stony Hills Prep so I have to stay on top. I'm getting out of the projects, and when I do—I'm never looking back."

The newness of her relationship with Carson must have worn off, I decide. I'm glad to hear she's back in her books. Rhyann is smart. Not as smart as she believes she is, but she's not dumb.

We talk for a few minutes more before ending the call.

I leave the bedroom, taking my cell phone with me. Aunt Phoebe is feeling better, but she's not in the mood to cook, so Alyssa and Chance are making dinner.

I would offer to help them out, but I'm not in the mood. Instead, I go back to my room to do some reading before it's time to eat.

We wait for Uncle Reed to come home before sitting down to the table. Chance and Alyssa cooked spaghetti. Big surprise.

After dinner, Alyssa and I set up the Scrabble game. We normally play on Thursday nights, but Aunt Phoebe wanted to play tonight instead. She said this is how she wanted to spend Valentine's. With her family.

Chance comes into the dining room, the telephone glued to his ear. "Trina, I'm working tomorrow night."

Alyssa and I pretend we're not hanging on to his every word.

"I can't change shifts with anybody. You should've told me about this earlier. Can't we go on Saturday?"

Aunt Phoebe and Uncle Reed join us, taking our attention away from Chance's conversation.

"I hope y'all ready for a spanking," Alyssa says. "I'm feeling good about this game tonight."

"I hope you won't be too disappointed," I tell her. I've won at Scrabble the last three games and I'm looking to make another win this evening.

We gather around the table, waiting on Chance to finish his phone call. He joins us a few minutes later. I can tell from his expression that he and Trina must have gotten into an argument. He always gets this pitiful look whenever she's mad with him.

The game begins with Uncle Reed forming a word on the board. Aunt Phoebe is next.

When Alyssa's turn comes, she spells out the word P-A-T-A. I'm like, "What is this?"

She gives me this Cheshire cat grin and says, "It means 'leg' in Spanish." Holding up a Spanish-English dictionary, Alyssa adds, "Check it out if you don't believe me."

Chance looks over at his parents. "Are we playing an international version of Scrabble?"

"We never said we wouldn't," Alyssa argues. "Divine's used French words before, and Italian."

"Let's do it," Aunt Phoebe suggests. "What's the worst that can happen? We learn another language."

My turn comes and I'm so ready. I spell out C-H-A-G-R-I-N. "How you like that?"

My smugness is temporary. The next two hands don't really do anything for me. Alyssa and Chance, on the other hand, are having a great night. Playing Scrabble is fun. It's the family time that I enjoy most since we really have a good time.

I have two messages from Madison and one from Mia when I check my phone later. I try Mia back but she doesn't answer—probably on the phone with Tim.

I shower and put on my pajamas and settle down in bed before calling Madison back. His sister answers the phone.

"I'm on the phone right now, Divine. I'll tell Madison to call you when I get off."

She clicks off before I can even get a word out of my mouth. It's times like this I wish Madison had been born an only child. His parents still refuse to allow him to get a cell phone, which is so totally crazy.

Everybody owns a cell phone these days.

I WAKE UP in a foul mood on Thursday morning. Mostly because I didn't get a chance to talk to Madison about our relationship last night. School is just not the place to discuss something so serious. We're back together but there are still some things we need to talk about.

Alyssa blows through my door, asking, "Divine, can I borrow one of your white shirts?"

"Sure," I mumble.

She practically dives into my closet. I continue making up my bed while Alyssa hunts for the perfect top for whatever she's wearing.

"I think I'll wear this one," she announces, holding up a Juicy Couture white T.

"Don't spill anything on it," I tell her. "It's one of my favorite tops and I don't want it ruined."

Alyssa eyes me. "What's up with you? You look like you're not happy about something."

"I can't stand Madison's sister. That witch stays on the telephone. I wish they'd get a second line or let him get a cell phone."

"She probably feels the same way when you and Madison are on the phone. Y'all stay on it for hours."

"We do not. Besides, whose side are you on?"

"I'm on your side, Divine. But you do have to consider that there are times when you and Madison talk for a long time."

"Then she should get a cell phone or something. Isn't she like in college or something?"

Alyssa shrugs. "I don't know."

"The reason Madison and I stay on the phone is because we have to make up for lost time."

She laughs. "His sister is probably doing the same thing."

"Marcia is just mean."

I march over to my closet and pull out the corduroy skirt and shirt I plan on wearing today. "Is your mom feeling better this morning?" I inquire.

"She said she was. She sounds a little stuffy though."

"I hope I don't catch it. The last thing I need is a cold or the flu."

We finish getting dressed and style our hair before heading to the kitchen to grab a bowl of cereal and some toast, which I eat as fast as I can. I'm so ready to leave for school. I want to see Madison.

Mom surprises me with a phone call. "Hon, I didn't get a chance to call y'all yesterday. Happy belated Valentine's Day. I'm so sorry."

"Mom, it's okay," I assure her. "I know you're busy. Besides, I did get the card and the gift card to Neiman's. I'm happy. We're all happy with our gifts. Did you find the present we left for you?" Alyssa, Chance, and I had put our moneys together to buy a really nice gift for Mom.

"Yeah. Miss Eula gave it to me. I love the watch. It's beautiful. Thank you, and please tell Alyssa and Chance that I love it."

I give Mom a quick update of what's happening in my life. She has to go and so do I, so we promise to catch up later.

We leave for school. My mood's a little better since talking to my mom. She's working on a new movie in Atlanta. At least this time she's not far away from home.

I am a little disappointed when I don't see Madison waiting for me. Stephen is there on the corner.

"Madison told me to tell you that he'll see you at school. He had to meet with his science teacher this morning."

That makes me feel better. I didn't know what to think initially. I don't want to go all paranoid, but I am being a little more cautious this time around. I was really hurt when Madison broke up with me. Now that he wants me back, I'm taking my time because I'm not sure whether he's for real. I'm just not gonna get played a second time.

chapter 7

I find Madison standing around laughing and talking with a bunch of boys near my first-period class. "I thought you had a meeting with one of your teachers. That's what Stephen told me."

"I did. I just came over here not too long ago. I didn't want to miss seeing you."

"Did Marcia tell you that I called last night?"

He shakes his head no. "Naw, she didn't tell me." A flash of anger washes over his expression. "Man, I hate that girl sometimes. I asked her if you'd called. She told me no."

"Well, Marcia lied. I did call you because I wanted to talk to you some more about our relationship. I really didn't want to do it while we're in school though."

"I can meet you afterwards," Madison offers.

81

I shrug in resignation. It's probably the only opportunity I'll have. Who knows if I'll be able to reach him tonight. Especially if that lying sister of his is at home. "I guess that'll have to do."

"Is it good news or are you going to break my heart?"

"Madison, I'd never try to hurt you. It's not bad news but we do have a lot to discuss." I glance over my shoulder before adding, "And I just don't want to do it here at school. *Too many ears.*"

"We can talk after school, or if you want, I can call you later this evening."

"Saturday is the baby shower for Trina and Chance," I announce.

Madison looks at me in surprise. "Chance is gonna hang around for the shower?"

I shrug. "I don't know. Probably, but I'm sure Aunt Phoebe is going to make him. She's making Uncle Reed come."

"I don't remember getting my invitation."

I meet Madison's gaze. "Like you really want to come to a baby shower."

"I'd come."

I chuckle. "You're so full of it."

We talk for a few minutes more before I make my way to class. I'm already longing for the bell to ring signaling the end of the school day. I'm not in the mood for education. I'm already wishing it were Friday, even though it's tomorrow. I'm just ready for the weekend.

Thankfully the day passes quickly.

Madison calls me around eight thirty.

"So what do you want to talk about?" he questions.

"Madison, I know we're back together and everything, but we need to clear up some things."

"Like what?"

"I've been doing a lot of thinking about us. Madison, I care a lot for you, but I can't let you treat me the way you did. I'm not going out like that again."

"Divine, I'm sorry. I'm more mature now and you don't have to worry about me ever doing that again. I won't ever hurt you—I promise. Girl, you don't know how much I prayed about us getting back together. I don't mean to sound like a punk . . ."

"You don't sound like a punk," I assure him. "But before you get too happy—we need to really talk about some stuff. Madison, I'm not going to have sex with you. It's the farthest thing on my mind. I need you to understand that. If you can't handle being with me and being celibate, we don't need to get back together."

"Why do you want to be celibate, Divine? Is it because it's what your aunt and uncle says you have to do?"

"It's because I don't want diseases; I don't want to get pregnant; but mostly I want my wedding night to be special. I want the man I marry to be the only one who knows that much about me. The other thing is that this is the way God wants it. I'm not trying to go all Holy Roller on you, but I'm also not trying to get on God's bad side."

"You're really serious about this, aren't you."

"Yeah. I am."

"I just want to be with you, so whatever you decide is cool with me."

Madison and I stay on the phone for nearly two hours. Marcia keeps interrupting our conversation by picking up one of the other extensions. I think she's hoping that her actions will irritate us to the point that we'll just get off the phone.

Not a chance.

It's payback time.

I'm FORCED TO get up at nearly the crack of dawn on Saturday because Aunt Phoebe wants Alyssa and me to help with decorating the house and getting it ready for Chance and Trina's baby shower.

As far as I'm concerned, this could've waited until a couple of hours before the party. I considered saying this to Aunt Phoebe, but I really don't want to get on my aunt's bad side.

I glance down at the balloons littering the floor in blues, yellows, and greens. Trina's having a boy so Aunt Phoebe said we didn't need any pink. I almost shouted with joy because I hate that color.

I bend down and pick up a green one, holding it in my hand and thinking, If I have to blow up another balloon, I'll scream.

Next on my list is the banner. Alyssa designed it—she should hang it. At least that's what I'm thinking.

"Chance, can you hang up the banner over here?" I ask just as he's about to walk past me.

"This baby is half-mine, you know. Why am I doing all this stuff for the baby shower?" he says as he begins to hang the banner.

"Because it's for you and Trina," I point out. "All you've done is hang this banner and blow up like two balloons. Stop whining."

"Why do people go through all this stuff just to give presents— you can just give me the gifts. I don't need all this."

"It's like a birthday party. I love parties myself. Your baby's getting his first one before he even arrives."

"It's not much longer," Chance says.

I glance over at him. "Are you getting nervous?"

He gives me this look like I've just asked him a really stupid question before answering, "Yeah. It's not gonna be that easy with a baby."

"I can't see you with a baby. You're just so . . . so goofy. I hope you don't mess around and drop him on his head or something." I chuckle.

"I'm not gonna drop Joshua. And I'm not goofy."

"Joshua? You're naming the baby Joshua?"

Chance nods. "Mama likes the name and so did Trina's mom."

I understand totally. Both grandmothers must have bullied them into giving the baby a biblical name. Chance and Trina probably only agreed to it because they're still feeling guilty for having sex.

Aunt Phoebe comes into the family room to check on my decorations. "Ooh, this looks nice," she says. "Divine, you did a beautiful job."

"I hung up the banner," Chance tells her.

"I like it." Aunt Phoebe embraces him. "Just think . . . little Joshua will be here soon. I can't wait to see that little angel."

Humph. A few months ago she was still having hissy fits, as Alyssa calls them, over the fact that her little boy was having a child before he was married.

Aunt Phoebe gives me a hug. "You really did a wonderful job, sugar. This place looks like a nursery."

"That's what you wanted me to do, right?"

She nods. "I love the teddy bears everywhere."

"Just remember these are from my collection and I'll be checking the guests' bags before they leave. I'm keeping my teddies. They love me and I love them."

Aunt Phoebe laughs.

My mind travels to my little brother, Jason, who lives in Atlanta with his grandmother. The last time I saw him was at his second birthday party in January. He's getting so big. I make a mental note to schedule another visit with him. With Jerome being in jail and his mother passed away—I feel like he needs me in his life. Even though he has a different mother, it doesn't matter to me. I love him like crazy.

I'll soon be having another sibling. Jerome's wife is four months along now. She's due in July. Ava tries to be real nice to me and she wants me to come spend some time with her. I said I would, but the truth is that I'm not exactly crazy about her. I'm still mad over her suing Mom for knocking her out and breaking her nose.

Talk about drama.

My thoughts are placed on hold when Alyssa finds me.

"Ooh, it looks nice in here," she says.

"You actually sound like you're surprised."

Alyssa's eyes travel to mine. "I can't believe you're actually awake. We didn't get to bed until almost one."

"Sssh, don't say that too loud. Aunt Phoebe will have a fit."

"She already knows. That's why she got us up so early."

"Are you serious?"

She nods.

"Aunt Phoebe goes to bed at ten o'clock every night unless she and Uncle Reed are out. How is it that she always knows what's going on all the time?"

"Mama says it's a mother's thing. She said we'll get it when we have children."

"I'm never having kids," I declare. "I'm going to be a fashion model until I'm too old to do it, then I'm going to be a fashion designer or work as a fashion editor for *Cosmopolitan* magazine."

"So if you and Madison get married and he wants to have a child—you're gonna say no?"

"He doesn't want children either."

"Did he tell you that?"

"Not really. We don't talk about getting married and stuff, like you and Stephen. Madison and I are just taking it one day at a time."

"Whatever," Alyssa mutters. "You be on the internet with me planning our weddings. You not fooling me."

"I want to get married one day—not have children."

"I think they come together."

"Only if you want it to," I counter.

Our discussion changes when Uncle Reed walks into the family room. He compliments our work before heading to the kitchen. He's making breakfast this morning. I love my uncle but he can't cook too well.

"What are you about to make?" I inquire.

"Hotcakes and sausage. Your aunt has a taste for some."

I glance over at Alyssa. Uncle Reed can make decent pancakes, but he always burns the sausage. I'm not in the mood for bad food, so I offer, "I'll cook the sausages for you."

"I thought you like blackened meat," Uncle Reed says with a laugh.

"It depends on whether it's actually supposed to be blackened." In the kitchen, I pull out Aunt Phoebe's large frying pan, setting it down on the stove top.

After I survive breakfast, I leave for my tae kwon do class. I'm not missing it today because I get my blue belt. Uncle Reed will be there and so will Mom. She's driving down from Atlanta—only she can't stay for Trina's baby shower. She's bringing some gifts so that I can give them to Trina.

Parents have crowded the visitors' area of the classroom with cameras, watching proudly as their children demonstrate the moves needed to step up in rank. I glance over my shoulder to where Mom and Uncle Reed are sitting before stepping up to perform my techniques that will qualify me for my next rank. My performance includes a kicking routine and one-step sparring, board-breaking.

When the ceremony ends, I remove my old belt along with the other students and put the new one in its place while our parents cheer and applaud.

"Congratulations, baby girl," Mom tells me. "I know how badly you wanted this. I'm very proud of you."

"I messed up when I was doing my spinning hook-kick."

Uncle Reed embraces me. "I think you did a great job, Divine."

Master Lee comes over and tells Mom how proud he is of me and how much he enjoys having me as a student.

When he moves on to the next student, Mom says, "You need to call Master Hughes and tell him about your blue belt."

I nod in agreement. "I will."

Uncle Reed and I walk Mom to her car.

She pulls out a big brown bag from Bloomingdale's. "This is for Trina."

I peer into the truck. "Nothing for me?"

Mom laughs. "No. I give to you every single day of your life."

"Except today," I tease. "Mom, you're slacking off."

"Give me a hug, baby girl. I need to get going."

I embrace my mom before saying good-bye.

When Uncle Reed and I return home, Aunt Phoebe congratulates me on my new belt before taking the Bloomingdale's big brown shopping bag filled with presents from me and sends us off to get ready before the guests start to arrive.

I am so through when I walk out of my room twenty minutes later and find Aunt Phoebe dressed in a bright pink jumpsuit. She even managed to find a matching headband. Frowning, I ask, "What do you have on? Even if it were fashionable, you have on the wrong color. Trina's having a boy."

"What's wrong with what I have on? The pants are long enough."

"It's not cute, Aunt Phoebe. I've told you that everything you see in the stores is not meant to be worn. Some things are just there to decorate the hangers. Nothing more."

"I happen to like my jumpsuit."

Alyssa strolls out of her bedroom. Taking a long look at her mother, she says, "Mama, I hope you are about to change clothes."

"For two people who don't have a penny to buy clothes for me, y'all got too many opinions about what I wear."

"We'd gladly do the shopping, Aunt Phoebe," I say. "I've been telling you that from the moment I stepped foot in this house."

"Mama, please change," my cousin pleads. "You don't need to wear that."

"Fine," Aunt Phoebe utters. "I'll just slip on a plain black dress."

"You'll feel so much better in it," I assure her.

Aunt Phoebe looks like she's mad enough to take me out of this world.

I take a step backward.

Half an hour before the party, a very pregnant Trina waddles into the house behind her parents, Mr. and Mrs. Winston.

"You look like you're ready to have that baby right this minute," I tell her, then realize that I probably shouldn't have told her that. I know how sensitive I am about my weight, so with her looking like a human beach ball, I'm sure I must have offended her.

"I am," she confirms. "Girl, I don't know what to do with myself. I'm so ready for this boy to come."

I feel a sense of relief that Trina doesn't appear to be offended by my words. I can't help but stare at her because she's like HUGE. Changing the subject, I ask, "Mia's still coming to the shower, right?"

Trina nods. "Yeah. She said she was going to try and get here early."

"You're supposed to sit in this chair," I tell Trina, pointing to the wing chair. "Aunt Phoebe wants to make sure you're the center of attention and that you're comfortable."

"Mrs. Matthews is so nice." Lowering her voice to almost a whisper, Trina continues, "I was so sure she was going to hate me when she found out I was having a baby."

"Oh, she was hot," I say. "She had a serious hissy fit."

"I know. She couldn't have been no worse than my own mama. I thought she was gonna kill me for sure when she found out I was pregnant."

"They all seem very excited now," I tell her. "Aunt Phoebe can hardly talk about anything else these days."

"I guess it's because the baby's coming no matter what." Trina runs a hand over her belly. "I hope everybody will love him."

"They will. I think they must love him already. Look at all this stuff." I eye her belly. "I can see him moving around." Placing a hand to her stomach, I ask, "Are you excited, little Joshua? I want you to know that I didn't have a thing to do with picking that name out for you. So when you get here, don't get mad at me. This is your cousin Divine."

Trina cracks up with laughter. "Don't you go starting no trouble. I love the name Joshua."

"Yeah, right." I don't believe her. "You and Chance probably picked out the name to make peace with your parents. Joshua is such an *old* name."

"Joshua is a strong name and means 'Jehovah saves.' Some say it means the Lord's salvation," Aunt Phoebe says when she enters from the kitchen. I keep forgetting she has the hearing of a dog.

"I still say it's a real old name for such a new little baby. I think you should wait until he gets here to see if he really looks like a Joshua. You can call him Chance Jr."

"I wanted to do that, but Chance didn't want a junior," Trina states. "He did agree to Joshua Michael because both of our dads have Michael as a middle name."

"He'll probably go by Michael then. I don't think he's going to like Joshua for a name."

Aunt Phoebe declares, "His name is going to be Joshua and

he'll use his birth name until he's grown enough to change it. That's all I got to say on the matter."

I glance over at Trina and smile. "I guess that's that."

She nods in agreement.

Chance comes in and takes a seat beside Trina, rubbing her belly. I catch Aunt Phoebe watching them and shaking her head, leading me to assume she's not as okay about this as I first assumed. She's just trying to make peace with the situation.

Uncle Reed is in his office when I pass by. I backtrack and knock on the open door.

"C'mon in, Divine," he tells me. "What can I do for you?" Uncle Reed asks when I take a seat on the sofa.

"I always hear you talking about how God loves us unconditionally. I think I really get it now. I was just in the family room with Trina and Aunt Phoebe. Chance came in and he sat down beside Trina and started rubbing her stomach. I saw Aunt Phoebe watching them, and for a moment she looked so hurt and so sad . . . but then she smiled. She loves Chance so much that even though she's hurt by his situation, she still wants the best for him and she's going to be there for him. This is the way God feels about us, right?"

Uncle Reed nods. "No matter what we do, God is always there for us."

"Does He really feel hurt like us?"

"I'm sure He does. God loves us so much that He sent His only son down here to die for us."

"That's some crazy love. I don't know if I'd ever send a child of mine to a world like this."

"So you can imagine the magnitude of God's love for us. We turn our backs on Him, rejecting Him and His laws—yet God never abandons us. We are truly a blessed people."

I hope Uncle Reed isn't about to preach. The shower will be starting soon and I don't intend to miss a minute of it. I suddenly feel guilty. God sent His only son and here I am wanting to rush out and join a party.

"Uncle Reed, God made a grand sacrifice for us—His son died for our sins. What does He really want from us? I mean, really want."

"Divine, God wants us to love Him fully and completely. We first have to really understand the impact of sin and recognize that it hurts God most of all. The Bible describes God as grieving over His lost and sinful creation. Not just in general either, but for each and every time one of us turns his or her back on Him."

I change my position on the sofa as Uncle Reed continues, "Then once we fully grasp what God has saved us from, our attitude of thankfulness and service to God will be a natural outflowing. He wants us to willingly open our hand and receive what we all know we need—forgiveness."

"I really get it now. It took me seeing how Aunt Phoebe was feeling when watching Chance and Trina." I stand up and head to the door. "Uncle Reed, please don't mention this conversation to her. I don't want to make Aunt Phoebe mad with me."

He smiles. "She wouldn't be upset about our talk, but I won't say anything."

"Thanks. I appreciate it. She's already an emotional wreck and I don't want to make it worse."

"Who's an emotional wreck?" Aunt Phoebe asks.

I glance back at Uncle Reed.

Aunt Phoebe eyes me. "What's going on?"

"Nothing. I was just having a little talk with Uncle Reed. I'm ready to get this shower started. Have all the guests arrived?"

"Most of them have. We're still waiting on Mia and Trina's aunt Sarah."

"I'll give Mia a call," I say, pulling out my cell phone. "I thought she'd be here by now."

Where are you, Mia? I wonder.

AFTER THE GUESTS leave, Trina, Alyssa, and I sit outside on the porch drinking hot chocolate and braving the chilly temperature.

"I can't believe Mia didn't show up to the baby shower. I got some words for that girl," Trina fusses.

"I called her cell phone a few times but it kept sending me to voice mail." I hand Aunt Phoebe a couple of plates. "I thought maybe she was just running late."

Shaking her head in confusion, Trina says, "I don't get it. I talked to Mia last night and she told me she would be here for my shower. I don't know what's been going on with her lately. She's been acting different."

I don't say a word. I promised Mia that I wouldn't be spreading her business around, and I intend to keep that promise. I can't be sure but I have a strong suspicion that Tim might be the reason that Mia didn't show up for the shower.

"She has been acting kind of distant since she started going with Tim," Trina says.

"What do you think about him?" I ask.

She shrugs. "He's okay I guess. Not too friendly, but then I don't really know him that well."

"I don't care for him," Alyssa blurts. "He looks like a gang-banger. I heard that's why his mama sent him to Temple to live with his grandmother."

"He's in a gang?" I ask.

"I don't know about that—I just heard he was hanging with some gang members and that's why he moved here from Birmingham."

When Trina tries to call Mia from her cell but gets voice mail as well, it makes me feel a little better. I thought maybe she was avoiding me.

"Trina and I are going to the movies tonight," Chance announces. "Y'all wanna come with us?"

"Yeah," Alyssa and I say in unison.

"We're leaving around six because we're getting something to eat first. *Be ready* or we're leaving without you."

Mia calls Trina on her cell.

"I thought you were coming to the shower. What happened?"

After listening a moment, Trina says, "I thought you were my girl. You stood me up for Tim. I see how you do friends."

Alyssa and I exchange looks. Trina is hot with Mia. I don't blame her though—I'd feel the same way. It's not like your friend has a baby shower every day. She and Trina are supposed to be BFFs. None of us can understand what's going on with Mia. I can't believe she's forgetting about her friends all because of Tim. He don't look that good.

Trina hands me her cell phone. "Mia wants to talk to you."

"Hello."

"Trina's really upset with me, huh?"

"Yeah," I say. "Wouldn't you be?"

"Can you talk to Trina, please? I wasn't trying to ditch her shower. Tim came over right before I was fixing to leave and he needed to talk. He was upset and I didn't want to leave him like that. I was trying to calm him down."

"So he's more important than your best friend?"

"No. That's not what I'm saying. Dang! It's not like Trina and I never see each other. We live across the street from each other."

"She wanted you here for the shower, Mia. It's a big deal. Look, we're all going to the movies tonight. Why don't you meet us at Spinners? We're eating there first."

"What time?"

"Are you really planning on showing up? *Without Tim, if possible.* Alyssa and I won't have any boyfriends following us around."

"I'll be there," Mia says. "I need to make up with Trina."

"I CAN'T BELIEVE you invited her," Trina complains when I tell her that Mia's joining us. "She didn't come to my shower—she's not gonna show up tonight."

"She'll be here," I say, scanning the menu. "Mia knows she hurt you and she wants to make it right."

"Humph. That won't happen anytime soon."

"Give Mia a chance," I implore Trina. "She just got caught up in Tim's drama. You know how that happens."

Trina takes a sip of her water. "I wouldn't miss my best friend's baby shower. Only sickness or death would keep me away."

Mia walks up to the table. She waves at me and Alyssa before saying, "I'm so sorry, Trina. I didn't mean to let you down like that."

"This was an important day for me and you weren't here for me."

Alyssa and I move over so that Mia can sit down. I give her my menu. I know what I'm ordering.

Mia is still trying to make up with Trina. "I messed up and I'm sorry. Trina, can't we find a way to get past this? You're my girl."

"I'm still mad with you for not coming to my baby shower," Trina states with a serious attitude. "You know how important it was. It's gon' take me a while to get over it."

The waitress comes over to take our orders.

"Trina, I explained to you why I couldn't come," Mia says when the waitress leaves the table.

"You don't get it, Mia," Trina snaps. "I'm supposed to be your friend. I've known you a whole lot longer than Tim. You can't make him your whole life, Mia. I'll still be around when he's long gone."

Alyssa and I exchange looks. Trina's about to tell Mia off and we have front-row seats.

"I understood when all you wanted was to be around Chance. I used to sit on the phone with you for hours listening to you talk about him. I didn't complain. Trina, I was happy for you."

"It's not the same thing, Mia. This was my baby shower. You could've come and left early or just arrived late. But you didn't show up at all. Divine called you and you wouldn't even answer the phone. You could've at least called to say you weren't coming."

"I didn't want to upset you."

Trina uttered a string of curses, shocking all of us. Glaring at Mia, she says, "Girl, you got me cussing up in here—I'm so mad at you."

Mia starts to tear up. "I said I was sorry. I can't go back and change anything, Trina."

Our food arrives.

Trina and Mia hardly touch theirs. The rest of us have no problem throwing down. Chance eats his meal and half of Trina's burger.

Alyssa breaks the heavy silence by saying, "You two have been friends a long time. Don't let something like this tear you apart."

"My sister's right," Chance states. "Don't break up a friendship over a shower. Trina, I know how much this means to you, but Mia is your friend. You know she cares about you."

"I really do," Mia tells her. "I messed up and I am sorry."

Trina runs a hand over her belly. Shrugging in resignation, she says, "We have been through a lot together. This is the first time you've ever really let me down. I'm sorry, too, for being so selfish. I probably would've done the same thing if it was me and Chance, but I would've called you to let you know I couldn't make it."

The tension in the air has evaporated, leaving us to enjoy the rest of our evening.

chapter 8

The weekend ends entirely too quickly for me. It's Monday already and time to go back to school. I groan as I climb out of bed, so not wanting to go back to Temple High. I've got two tests scheduled and I don't feel prepared even though I've studied all of two hours for both.

I slip on a pair of skinny AG Adriano Goldschmied jeans and a Juicy Couture long-sleeve T-shirt. Normally, I try to wear my hair down, but this morning I'm just not feeling it. I pull it back into a ponytail.

Thankfully, I'm cute enough to pull off a bad-hair day.

After slipping on my brown leather designer boots, I finish off my look with a chunky necklace and matching earrings.

Alyssa is in her room playing with her hair when I walk in. I scrutinize her for a moment before saying, "Naah . . . I don't think you need to wear your hair like that. Just do like I did—pull it into a ponytail."

She's gonna drive me crazy with those braids. Aunt Phoebe allowed Alyssa to get her hair braided, and since then my cousin can't seem to keep her hands out of her hair. They look good on her but I wish she'd try to focus on something else—anything else.

"Hurry up, Alyssa. I'd like to have breakfast before we have to leave for school."

"Go on and eat then. I'll be there in a minute."

She doesn't have to tell me twice. I leave Alyssa's room and rush down the hallway toward the kitchen. Aunt Phoebe and Uncle Reed are already seated at the table eating. I join them. "Good morning."

"Morning, Divine," they say in unison.

I reach for a biscuit and place it on the empty plate in front of me. "I could smell the bacon you cooked all the way in my room," I tell Aunt Phoebe.

"It woke me up this morning," Uncle Reed says.

I put two pieces on my plate, then ask, "Could you please pass the scrambled eggs, Aunt Phoebe?"

"Sure." She hands me a medium-size bowl of fluffy scrambled eggs.

After spooning some on my plate, I say grace before diving in. I love bacon and I especially love Aunt Phoebe's hot, buttery biscuits. She and Mom both use my grandmother's recipe. They're light and practically melt in your mouth. My aunt fries the bacon to perfection. Not too hard and not too soft.

Alyssa walks into the kitchen, Chance on her heels. "Y'all eating without us?" she asks.

"We'd be starved if we had to wait on you," I say between bites.

"I know you not trying to talk. Miss I-can't-leave-the-house-without-my-makeup."

I laugh. "I'll be on time. As soon as I finish eating this bacon, I'm going to fix my face and be waiting by the door before you even sit down to eat."

"I'd like to see that," Uncle Reed mutters.

"Just wait and see." I push away from the table and stand to my feet. "I'll be at the front door in a few minutes."

Five after seven, I wait by the door for Alyssa and Chance.

"Told you sooo," I sing when they walk out to the foyer.

"There's a first time for everything," Alyssa says.

"Whatever."

I run into Mia on my way to my first-period class. I can tell right off that she's been crying because her eyes are red, swollen, and puffy.

"What's wrong?" I ask.

Shaking her head, she answers, "Nothing."

I can just look at her and tell she's lying. "Mia, c'mon . . . I can see that you've been crying. *Talk to me.*"

"I don't know what I keep doing wrong," she begins before bursting into another round of tears.

I pull her off to the side. "Mia, what are you talking about? Tell me what happened? Did Tim do something to you?"

"Why don't you mind your business?" a deep voice bellows from behind me. "What goes on between me and my girl ain't your concern."

I turn around to face Tim.

"Why don't you shut up?" I snap. "I'm talking to my friend."

"Well, she done talking with you." Reaching for her, he says, "C'mon, Mia. We got some things to discuss."

I step between them.

Ignoring Tim, I say, "Mia, let's go. We don't want to be late for class."

She wipes her face on her sleeve. "Divine, I'll see you there. Tim and I need to talk."

I have a bad feeling about leaving Mia so I say, "Sorry, but I'm not leaving without you."

"I'll be all right," she says in a low voice. "Please go, Divine."

Her eyes keep darting over to Tim and she looks scared to death.

"I'm not leaving."

Tim gets up in my face, yelling, "Girl, didn't you hear me? Mia and I got some things to work out."

"Then you'll just have to do it with me standing right here," I yell back. "And you better get out my face."

"You don't want to mess with me," he warns.

"Same here. I'm not scared of you."

"Then you more stupid than you look."

Did this fool just call me stupid? Oh, no, he didn't.

My hands on my hips, I say, "Boy, I got more sense than you can ever conceive of in that minuscule brain of yours." I can tell from his expression that he has no clue what "minuscule" means. I decide to give him some help. "It means tiny."

Tim looks like he's about to pounce on me, but Madison suddenly appears out of nowhere saying, "What's going on here? Divine, you okay?"

"You better talk to your girl. Tell her to stay out of my business."

Madison looks over at me. "Is he bothering you?"

"No. He's bothering Mia."

Tim mutters a curse. "Y'all better . . . c'mon, Mia. I ain't got time for these fools."

I grab Mia gently by the arm. "You're going to class. I know for a fact you have a test this morning, and you don't need to miss it. You know Mr. Houston won't let you take it if you're late."

"Yo, Mia . . ."

"Tim, why don't you chill out? You act like you can't be away from your girl more than two minutes. *Man up.*"

Tim flexes his arms, saying, "You need to get out my face, punk!"

I grab my boo by the hand. "Madison, you need to come with us. You know he's mean and crazy."

Tim shouts a stream of curses at me.

"Whatever," I reply. Loud enough for him to hear, I say, "Told you he was crazy."

"Divine, please don't do that," Mia pleads. "You don't want to make him angry."

"What is he going to do to me?" I huff.

"Just let me stay and talk to him. I can calm him down. When he's like this—he'll get in a fight and I don't want to see him kicked out of school. You know Mr. McPhearson don't like Tim. He told him if he gets in another fight, he's gone."

Serves him right, from where I'm sitting. I look forward to the day we won't have Tim walking around terrorizing everyone at school. "Mia—"

"No," she interjects. "Divine, go on to your class. I want to talk to Tim."

Madison and Tim look as though they are about to come to blows, so I take my boo by the arm, pulling him away. "Let's go. She wants to stay here with him. I don't have time for this mess. We need to get to class."

"I can't stand that dude," Madison mutters.

"The only person who seems to like him is Mia. Why, I don't know."

Mia doesn't show up for our fourth-period Spanish class. I

don't see her again until right before lunch. "Where have you been? Coach McCall knows that you were in school today. She's writing you up for skipping her class."

"Tim and I had a lot to talk about." She takes one look at my face and says, "I know you don't understand."

"I'm very surprised. You two are always together—don't you ever run out of stuff to say?"

"I love spending time with Tim. He's crazy about me. That's what we want, right? Men that are absolutely in love with us."

"Do you really?"

"Yeah. Why would you ask me that?"

"Because whenever I'm around you two, it looks like you're scared of him."

She broke into a short, nervous laugh. "That's stupid. I'm not afraid of Tim. He's my boo."

"How can you love somebody who scares you so much?"

"I just don't like when he gets angry. That's all. I'm not afraid of him and I wish you'd stop saying that."

"Whatever," I mutter. "Mia, I'm through with this discussion. You and Tim are tripping and I don't want to be a part of it."

"You made yourself part of it—we didn't invite you into our relationship."

I can't believe she went there with me. Mia has seriously been demoted. She's no longer a BF. She's just an associate at this point. I walk off without so much as another word to her.

AFTER SCHOOL ENDS, Mia has the nerve to confront me in the hallway. "Divine, I know you think you have all the answers, but you don't. Tim is right. You really need to stay out of our business."

"I'm really tired of having this discussion with you, Mia. But I want you to answer me one question. If I hadn't been there, what do you think he would have done?"

"He only wanted to apologize to me."

"You really believe that?"

Mia nods. "Yeah. I do. I know him a lot better than you do, Divine."

I shake my head in frustration. "He's really got you brainwashed. You are so not the Mia I used to know."

"No, he doesn't. You just don't like him. Well, for your information, Divine, he doesn't like you either."

Waving my hand in dismissal, I respond, "I really don't care whether he likes me. I *do* care about the way he treats you. Mia, what would you do if Madison was hitting on me and making me cry all the time?"

"I wouldn't like it, but if he's the boy you want to be with, I wouldn't try to stand in your way. I'm sure you know what you're doing. I would trust that."

"Then maybe you're not really my friend," I snap.

Mia releases a long sigh. "You don't understand."

"Oh, I understand. You're being abused by your boyfriend, Mia. And you're too scared to do anything about it."

"That's not what's happening."

"You keep on believing that," I snap, frustrated with Mia at this point. "I need to meet Alyssa."

"Divine, do you know what's going on with Mia?" Alyssa asks me while we're walking home.

"What are you talking about?"

"She seems to be acting funny lately. And Stacy told me that Mia's been skipping class."

I shrug in nonchalance. She's not my problem anymore. I tried to be a good friend but she rejected my help. Mia's on her own. "I guess she's all right," I answer. "She just needs to get rid of Tim."

THE NEXT DAY at school, I vow to stay as far away from Mia as possible. I'm not sure we're even associates anymore. She's really made me angry with her.

We're just about to walk into the building when I hear Alyssa say, "Oh my gosh! Look at Mia. She's got a black eye."

I glance over my shoulder.

"What do you think happened to her?"

I have an idea but decide not to put her on blast. I don't want to break my promise to Mia even though I think she's being stupid. I don't understand why she won't just break up with Tim and get him out of her life for good.

Mia walks over to where we're standing, her head down.

"What happened to you?" Alyssa questions. "Were you in a fight?"

She glances over at me before answering Alyssa. "I got jumped by these girls from Villa Rica. One of them thought I was messing with her boyfriend."

"Are you?" I ask.

"No."

Peering closer at Mia's eye, Alyssa wants to know, "You sure Tim's not seeing someone else?"

"He's not. This has nothing to do with him."

"I bet," I mutter.

Mia glares at me through her one good eye.

The bell rings.

"I'll see y'all later," Alyssa says. "I don't want to be late."

I confront Mia with her lies when we're alone. "You're something else. You're actually covering for that jerk."

"It was my fault, Divine."

"What do you mean this is your fault? What did you do to make Tim give you a black eye?"

"I was talking to this boy I used to go with. Tim saw us and thought I was cheating on him. We got into an argument and he was about to walk off. I grabbed his arm and . . . Divine, it was just his reflex. He doesn't like to be grabbed like that."

"I'm still waiting for the part that's your fault."

"It's just a big misunderstanding. That's all."

I shake my head. "Not it's not. Mia . . . you need to face the truth." Having said that, I leave her standing there. I'm so angry with her—how could she let him punk her like that?

chapter 9

After we finish our homework, Alyssa and I ride over with Chance to see Trina. She's been calling us and complaining of boredom, so we thought we'd go cheer her up. Chance is taking her some money, then he has to be on his way to work. Aunt Phoebe's going to come pick us up around eight.

"How are you feeling?" I ask, taking a seat on the sofa beside her. "Besides being so bored."

"Okay," Trina answers. "I'm just ready for this baby to come. Girl, I can't wait to get my body back."

Alyssa picks up a slice of pizza. Mrs. Winston ordered it for us to eat during our visit. "It feels weird, doesn't it?" she wants to know.

Trina nods. "I still can't believe there's a baby inside me."

Turning my lips downward, I say, "I can't believe the way it's coming out."

"I don't even want to think about that."

"You need to start thinking about it," I state. "The baby's coming any day now."

"Chance is so scared."

"I am, too," Trina confesses. "I'll be glad when the baby's here. I can't wait to see my little boy."

"I hope he doesn't have a big head like Chance," Alyssa states with a laugh. "Girl, if he does, I feel sorry for you."

We all laugh.

"Have you talked to Mia?" Trina asks me. "I called her last night but she hasn't called me back yet. It's getting harder and harder to reach that girl."

"We saw her today at school."

"She's got a black eye," Alyssa announces. "She said some girls jumped her from Villa Rica High."

Trina looks from me to Alyssa. "When did this happen?"

"She said yesterday," I answer.

"You sound like you don't believe her."

"Trina, I don't know what to believe. Mia's not herself since she started messing with Tim. You know that."

"He's probably cheating on her with a girl from Villa Rica. That's why Mia got jumped on."

Alyssa agrees.

I don't respond because I know better, and I hate it because I can't say or do anything about it. I've never felt so helpless.

Trina pulls out all the clothes she's gotten for the baby. They're cute and all, but I'm just not into the whole baby thing. I'm so bored.

Eight o'clock can't come quick enough for me. I'm so ready to get away from this talk of babies, babies, and more babies. I'm beginning to break out in hives just at the mention of them—perhaps I'm allergic.

Aunt Phoebe arrives and I'm so happy I could kiss her. I don't, of course.

I rush to my feet, saying, "Trina, it's good seeing you, girl. Call me."

Alyssa stands up and crosses the room. "I'll talk to you later."

Aunt Phoebe and Trina's mom stand near the door talking while Alyssa and I patiently wait for them to finish. My cell phone rings.

It's Madison, so I answer. "Hey, I'm on my way back to the house. I'll give you a call when I get there."

My number suddenly becomes a hotline. It rings again—this time Mimi is the caller. I tell her the same thing, promising to call her within the hour. The next caller is Rhyann. I let this one roll over to voice mail.

"Somebody sure is blowing your phone up," Alyssa says.

"It's not just one person," I respond.

Her phone rings, bringing Aunt Phoebe's attention to her. "Y'all and these cell phones," she utters.

Trina's mom chimes in, "I thought they were supposed to be for emergencies. At least that's why my child said she wanted one."

"Kids use them now for everything," Aunt Phoebe states. "I guess it saves on having to put an extra phone line into the house."

When we arrive home twenty minutes later, Mom calls to tell us that she's taking us to Martinique, French West Indies, for spring break.

Alyssa's ecstatic. Chance was invited to go with us but, with the baby coming, he needs to stay close to home. I can tell he's disappointed even though he's trying to hide it.

As soon as I get off the phone with Mom, I call Mimi and tell her. This year spring break runs the same week for both our schools. She's planning to talk her mom into coming to Martinique so that we can vacation together. I'd love for Rhyann to join us, but I know her aunt probably won't let her come. She's tight when it comes to money. At least that's what Rhyann always says.

Madison's less than thrilled when I share my news with him. It's not something he wanted to hear. It's not like I can actually spend any time with him anyway. I'd be sitting over at my aunt and uncle's house while he's at his house talking on the telephone. Not my idea of a great spring break.

I take a few minutes to write Jerome a letter, just to let him know that I'm thinking of him. He asked me to call Ava in his last note to me. It's been a week since I received it, but I haven't done it.

What would I say to her?

I want to talk to Mom about it, but I'm not sure how to bring it up. I don't want to make her feel sad or upset her. Ava is definitely not one of her favorite people in the world. Anytime I've been around them, they seemed pretty civil to me, but the tabloids tell a much different story.

I'm so tired of seeing my parents' faces plastered all over those "supermarket rags," as Mom's assistant, Stella, calls them. I had hoped all the fascination with Jerome would've died down a long time ago, but it hasn't. Now they are doing a baby watch. As soon as Ava gives birth, my half brother or sister's photo will be plastered all over the media. At least Jason's been spared that trauma.

Every now and then, some of the kids at school try to say stuff about Jerome, but I ignore them. He's in prison. Everybody knows that, and while I'm not proud of it, he's still my father, and since I didn't pick him, there's not a whole lot I can do about that fact. I'm stuck with Jerome.

He's not so bad since getting locked up. In fact, I think prison has done a lot of good for him. Jerome writes to me weekly, he's studying his Bible, and he seems to really love Ava.

He seems to treat her so much better than the way he treated Mom. I have to admit that bothers me some. Mom keeps telling me that she wasn't perfect either, but I still lay most of the blame at Jerome's door.

My eyelids grow heavy and I can't seem to stop yawning.

I finish my letter and get ready for bed. I practically fall into bed, I'm so tired. My phone rings but I don't bother to see who's calling me. All I want to do right now is sleep.

AFTER WHAT SEEMS like an eternity, we are finally on our way to Martinique.

"It rains every day on the island," Mom tells us during the flight. "But it's beautiful there."

"Martinique is also home to an active volcano that erupted killing everyone in the town of Saint-Pierre except a man in jail," I say.

I chuckle at the horrified expression on Alyssa's face.

"Now you tell me something like that. While we're on the plane on our way there."

Mom gives me this look.

"What did I do?"

"You know what you did. It's not funny either."

I roll my eyes at Alyssa before slipping my headphones on. That girl has no sense of humor sometimes.

By the time our plane lands, I've forgiven Alyssa and we're back on speaking terms. I check my watch. Mimi's plane should be touching down in another ten minutes. I'm looking forward to seeing her.

Mom arranges for the driver to pick up our luggage.

I turn around as soon as I hear my name being called. My initial surprise turns to joy when I see Rhyann. "What are you doing here?" I ask her.

"Mimi's mom paid for me to come." She hugs me. "I'm so glad to see you, girl."

Mimi and I embrace. "We are going to have the best time ever," she tells me.

Alyssa and Rhyann are already laughing and talking. From the first time they met when Alyssa came to California with me, they've become friends. I don't mind because the only time they really talk is when we're all together. They might email each other every now and then, but Rhyann's closer to me. It's the same with Penny and Stacy. They like me well enough, but they are Alyssa's BFFs.

I glance around. "Where's my mom?"

"She and Mother are talking to the driver. I saw them walk outside a few minutes ago."

We walk outside to join them.

The driver packs our luggage into the trunk of the limo. We climb inside and settle down for the drive to a private villa Mom rented for our stay.

"I can't believe there's rush-hour traffic here, too," Rhyann says. "I was looking forward to getting away from that drama."

The first thing we do after arriving at the villa is change into swimsuits and jump into the pool.

"I'm so glad I have braids," Alyssa tells me. "I don't have to worry about my hair this week."

"I know. I wish I'd gotten some before we left."

Rhyann has her hair in braids, too, so only Mimi and I will be fussing with blow-dryers and curling irons for the next six days.

I pull Mimi off to the side. "So how are things between your parents?"

"They're on speaking terms now and Mother's not talking

about moving to England anymore. I'm not real sure what it all means yet."

"Sounds like they're trying to work it out to me."

Mimi shrugs in nonchalance. "I don't want to get my hopes up. You know?"

I nod in understanding.

We swim and lie out around the pool for the next couple of hours. When we finally decide to go back into the house, my stomach's growling up something awful. I check out the kitchen, surprised to find the pantry and refrigerator fully stocked.

Mom enters behind me. "I had the housekeeper do some shopping for us."

"Oh. I was wondering about all this food. I didn't know how long it had been here."

"There's some fruit in the fridge and some deli meat and cheese for sandwiches. Why don't you make some sandwiches? I'm sure the girls are hungry."

"They can make their own sandwiches. Mimi's way too picky for me to fix anything for her to eat. I'd have to hurt her feelings."

Mom laughs. "You're one to talk."

"Exactly. So why would I want to deal with someone like me?"

After lunch, we settle down in the media room to watch a movie. I catch Alyssa's eye and grin.

Our spring break is off to a wonderful start.

ALYSSA AND I return home the following Sunday, loaded down with souvenirs, some hot new clothes, and lots of pictures from our time in Martinique.

"We had a great time," we tell Aunt Phoebe and Uncle Reed when they pick us up from Mom's house.

I call Madison as soon as I get home because we didn't talk much during our break. I know he's probably fit to be tied, as Aunt Phoebe says. I missed him but I wanted to really enjoy my friends. I don't get to see Mimi and Rhyann that often anymore. Hopefully, he'll understand.

But if not . . . oh, well. I'm not going to worry about it.

Marcia's on the phone so I know it's highly unlikely that I'll get a chance to talk to him this evening. For once, I'm too tired to complain.

The next morning, we head back to school, our vacation just a memory.

Madison and Stephen are waiting on the corner for us.

We hug our boyfriends in greeting.

"Did you try to call me last night?" Madison asks.

"Yeah. Marcia was on the telephone."

"I kept telling her that I had to use the phone. That girl . . . she gets on my nerves. She's been talking about moving out—getting her own place. I wish she would."

Me, too, I think to myself.

I see Mia and Tim as soon as I step on campus. She throws up her hand in a tiny wave but doesn't speak.

Whatever . . .

She tries to come over and say something to me during lunch, but I don't have a whole lot to say back.

"What's wrong with you?" she asks me finally.

"Don't go there," I respond.

"Why is everybody tripping over Tim? I don't do that with y'all."

"You don't want to go there with me either."

Mia is quiet for a moment as if searching for something to say. I help her out by asking, "What did you do for spring break?"

"Nothing. Just hung around the house. I heard you and Alyssa went to Martinique."

"We had a good time, too. My friends Mimi and Rhyann were there."

I tell her about all the cute boys we saw; how much fun we had shopping, swimming, and eating.

"Sounds like you had a lot of fun."

"We did," I confirm. "We're talking about going again next year. You know, like make it an annual event."

"Maybe I can save up my money and go with you the next time."

"Sure. I'd like for you to meet Rhyann and Mimi."

"I hear you talk about them so much. I feel like I already know them." Mia takes a sip of her soda. "Divine, I miss talking to you like this. We've been doing so much arguing—"

"You've been arguing," I correct her. "Not me. I've been trying to help you."

"The *point* is that I miss us."

I'm too proud to admit that I've missed Mia, too. When I've been hurt by someone who is supposed to be my friend or claims to care about me, I don't let them get as close to me until I know that they're really down for me. It might be wrong, but that's just the way I am.

The bell rings.

We leave the cafeteria, walking to fifth period. I can't wait for school to let out. I'm still in vacation mode and I need a nap.

Madison is waiting for me by the gym when I get out of my sixth-period class. "Hey," he greets. "I'm walking home with you and Alyssa today."

"Oh."

"Why you say it like that? Somebody else walking you home? You waiting on that Nicholas dude?"

I shake my head no. "Stop acting so jealous, Madison."

"Hey, guess what?"

"What?"

"I got me a job."

"Where?"

"I'll be working at McDonald's. I won't be able to walk with y'all sometimes. I'ma have to rush home so I won't be late for my job."

"How do you think you'll like working at McDonald's?" It's not the kind of place I'd consider working at. I don't tell Madison that because I don't want to hurt his feelings.

"It's a job. They'll be giving me a paycheck. I want to buy a car. My pop says if I save up some money, he'll match it and help me get one."

"He won't just buy you one?"

Madison shakes his head no. "My family's not all rich like yours. Pops says that if I have to pay for half the car, I'll take care of it."

"Oh" is all I can say in response. It's not that I'm too cute to work a regular job or that I think I'm too rich. My mom doesn't want me working a part-time job. She wants me to focus on my studies.

I get a text message from Mimi.

I had a gr8 time with u and Alyssa last week. I miss u already. U really need 2 move back to Cali.

Mimi

I text her back.

We had a fun time with u and Rhyann. Loads of fun. I'll b n Cali before u know it. I mis u 2.

Dee

Tuesday after school, I spend most of my time working on a project that's due Friday. I won't be able to work on it tomorrow because of choir rehearsal.

I like singing in the choir, but at times I wish I didn't. I'm missing some good TV shows that come on Wednesday nights. I record as many of them as I can, but it seems like I never get around to watching them.

I take a break at dinnertime but return to work on my project afterward.

Mia calls me around eight and we talk for almost an hour.

I'm stunned.

I haven't spoken to Mia on the phone in a minute. Not since we had that little disagreement over Tim. It's pretty clear to me that she's chosen him over her true friends. Like whatever . . .

Now we're sitting here, talking and laughing like nothing ever happened. I have to admit, I've missed her. Mia can be a lot of fun. The girl is crazy.

"Did he really say that?" she asks.

"Yeah. He was from New York, and, Mia, you should've seen him trying to get his mack on. It was too funny."

When our conversation draws to a close, Mia tells me, "I missed talking to you, girl."

"Me, too."

"I better get off this phone. I need to finish my homework before my parents kill me."

"I'll see you tomorrow," I say. "Oh, don't forget your PE clothes. We have to dress out."

Mia never mentioned Tim and neither did I. We seem to get along so much better when we don't talk about him. He's not a favorite subject of mine anyway.

We end our call and I return to my project, feeling much better about my relationship with Mia.

chapter 10

$\mathcal{O}ur$ friendship is once again tested when she calls me two days later. I'd just gotten home from school and was about to do my laundry.

"Divine, this is Mia."

"What's up?"

"I need a favor," she begins, her voice shaky. "Divine, I'm at the hospital. Can you come down? I don't want to be alone."

"Where are your parents?"

"They're home but I don't want to worry them."

Mia looked like she was fine during school. "What happened?"

"I was practicing a routine for cheerleading tryouts and hurt my arm. It's not a big deal but I don't like doctors."

"I need to ask my aunt Phoebe. Can you hold on?"

"Yeah."

"Aunt Phoebe, could you take me to the hospital please? Mia's there. She hurt her arm."

"Where are her parents?"

"I guess they weren't home," I lie. "Can I go be with her? She sounds scared."

"I'll drop you off, but if her parents aren't there by the time she's ready to leave, call here and one of us will pick you both up."

"I'll be there in a few minutes," I tell Mia.

During the ride to the hospital, I can't help but wonder if this really is an accident or has Tim been hitting on her again.

I don't see Mia in the waiting room so I check the information desk. Once I'm told where she is, I make my way to her.

I find her sitting alone, tears running down her face. I hand her a tissue before saying, "You know this means no more cheerleading for you. If you get hurt during the tryouts . . ."

She gives a short laugh. A few minutes later, her smile disappears and Mia suddenly gives me this real serious look. "Divine, thank you so much for coming out here to be with me. I really don't like doctors or hospitals."

Mia and I sit in the room waiting for someone to come check her out. "I think you broke your arm."

"All I know is that it hurts."

"What exactly were you doing or trying to do?"

"I was working on a routine for cheerleading practice. You still planning on trying out for next year?"

I shrug. "I don't know."

Deep down, I'm having some trouble believing that Mia got hurt during cheerleader tryouts.

"Why are you being so quiet?" Mia asks suddenly, breaking up the silence.

"Mia, I'm just worried about you."

She sighs. "What is it?"

"How did you really hurt your arm? I'm having a hard time believing that you broke it doing some stupid handspring."

"That's what happened, Divine."

Something in her tone makes me wonder otherwise. "I don't believe you."

"There you go again. You think Tim did this to me, don't you?"

"Didn't he? Mia, I'm your friend even though you don't like me telling you the truth about your boyfriend."

"Divine, my relationship with Tim is complicated."

I totally agree with Mia. It's probably the first true thing she's said when it comes to Tim. Mia suddenly falls back against the examination table, prompting me to question, "What's wrong, Mia?"

"I don't know. I just feel dizzy all of a sudden." She falls back on the hospital bed. "I feel sick."

I rush to my feet, and throwing the curtain to one side, I yell, "She needs a doctor. Hurry."

I'm almost knocked to the ground by a nurse in a rush to get to Mia. I make sure to stand out of the way while they get her situated on the bed.

Mia is taken to have X-rays done. I sit in the room waiting for her to return. I hear a buzzing and glance down. Mia's cell phone is vibrating. I reach down to get it and turn it off.

I note that it's Tim who's calling, and from the number of missed calls—he's been blowing up her phone. I'm tempted to answer and tell him off, but I don't. Instead, I call her mom and dad. They need to know what's going on with Mia.

They arrive twenty-five minutes later.

"Where is she?" they ask in unison.

Before I can respond, the orderlies roll Mia back into the little cubicle-size room.

"Baby, what happened?" her mother questions.

"I had an accident when I was practicing a cheerleading routine and I broke my right arm. The doctor said it was only broken in one place."

I can't believe she's lying about something so important. Tim broke her arm—I'm sure of it.

Mia's mom assumes that I was present when Mia hurt her arm. "Divine, how do you think you performed?"

Mia silently pleads with me to keep my mouth shut. "Okay, I guess," I mutter.

"You girls have to be careful. Making the cheerleading team is nice, but it's not the end of the world if you don't. Just do the best you can."

"Yes, ma'am."

Her parents walk outside the cubicle to speak with the nurse.

"Thanks so much, Divine," Mia whispers.

"Mia, you better hope my aunt and uncle don't say anything to your parents. We weren't together after school, and we definitely weren't trying out for cheerleading. In fact, I haven't seen you outside of school lately."

"I'm sorry about that."

"I don't care about that stuff." Rising to my feet, I move to stand beside the bed. "Mia, I need you to be totally honest with me. Did Tim do this to you? Was he having one of his tantrums?"

Her eyes dart to the curtain. "Divine . . . my parents are here. I don't want them hearing this stuff about Tim."

I decide to try another tactic to get Mia to be honest. "If you don't tell me the truth, I'm going to tell your parents that I wasn't there with you today."

"Divine, please don't do that. I told them that I was with you."

"That's why you wanted me to be here with you before you called them. Mia, I don't like lying to them."

"I'd do it for you."

"Mia, it's not about that. Somewhere deep inside you, don't you feel that Tim hurting you is wrong?"

She doesn't respond.

"Did you hear me?"

"Okay . . . Look, Divine . . . it was an accident."

"Tell me what happened."

"First, you need to understand that Tim didn't mean to break my arm. We got into an argument, and when I wanted to leave, well, he didn't like me walking off. He came after me and I slapped him. I got tired of him grabbing on me." Mia's eyes traveled to mine. "I shouldn't have slapped Tim. I'd never seen him so angry."

"What is it going to take, Mia?"

Her eyes fill with unshed tears.

"So what was it this time?" I ask. "What did you do to make him so mad?"

"It wasn't anything important. Tim thinks that every boy at Temple High wants to be with me. He's very jealous. This time it just got out of hand."

"I'd hate to think what he'd do to you if you really upset him."

Mia sighs. "You don't understand."

"No, it's you who doesn't get it. That boy is hurting you, Mia. *He's abusing you.*"

The doctor has to set Mia's arm.

"I've called my aunt," I announce. "She's on her way to pick me up."

"Divine, we would've taken you home."

"It's no problem. Aunt Phoebe's already on her way here. I'm going to wait out front for her. Mia, be careful with that arm."

"I'll give you a call sometime tomorrow," she tells me.

"Whatever," I mutter. I'm just too through with Mia. Tim's broken her arm and she's still defending him.

Why? What kind of hold does he have over Mia?

AUNT PHOEBE ARRIVES at the hospital to pick me up. "How's Mia?"

"She broke her arm. She's okay but she can forget about the cheerleading tryouts this year."

"Poor thing," Aunt Phoebe mutters. "I'm so sorry to hear that."

I don't talk much on the drive back to the house. I can't help but worry about Mia and the trouble I'll be in if my aunt and uncle find out we lied.

"Divine, you look troubled. Sugar, what's wrong?"

"I'm fine, Aunt Phoebe," I respond with a tiny smile. "I was just thinking about something."

"You were thinking pretty hard on it from the looks of it."

I don't respond, then ask, "Where's Alyssa?"

"She and Penny went to the mall with Stacy."

"I wish they'd told me they were going," I say. "I hate missing out on any opportunity to shop."

"You're in luck, sugar. We're on our way to meet them."

Her words brighten my mood.

"Divine, is there something else going on with Mia?"

"No, ma'am."

"You know that you can talk to me about anything."

"Aunt Phoebe, I know." I pray she doesn't keep asking me questions. I don't want to lie to her, but I can't put Mia on blast like that. Not after I gave her my word. I have to honor the BF code.

But Tim is abusing her.

Right now, I'm a little bit confused as to what to do about this situation. I don't want to break a promise, but I also don't want to see Mia continue to be abused. I glance upward.

Lord, I really need your guidance. I really don't know what to do. I don't want to make the wrong decision.

When we get to the mall, my mind is troubled to the point that I can't really enjoy shopping.

"You must be feeling sick or something," Alyssa says to me. "You haven't picked up one shirt or a pair of pants. What's up with that?"

"I can't believe I'm saying this, but I'm just not in the mood to shop."

Everyone suddenly stops walking and is staring me down.

"What?"

Penny shakes her head. "I can't believe I just heard you say that. I'm in shock."

Stacy agrees. "When you and Madison broke up, you were still able to go shopping. I've never seen you look so down."

I silently wish they'd just shut up. Aunt Phoebe hasn't said anything, but I'm sure she's listening and taking in every word. I'm so sure she'll be interrogating me when we get back to the house.

"There's nothing wrong with me," I state. "I'm just not in the mood to shop. *It happens.*"

Alyssa's still not convinced. "Maybe to other people, Divine. But not to you."

I send her a sharp look. I know she's probably confused by my attitude, but I have a lot on my mind right now. Coming to the mall was not the right decision for me. I should have gone straight home.

Nobody speaks a word to me as we walk around the mall, going from store to store. I'm so bored.

Madison calls me on my cell. While the others are in the Gap, I sit outside on a nearby bench talking to my boo.

"I called you earlier," he tells me. "I think your phone was off."

"I was at the hospital with a friend. You can't have your cell on when you're inside the building."

"What friend?"

I knew he was going to ask me that.

"It was Mia. She broke her arm." Not much point in lying since he'll see her around school in a cast.

"What happened to her?"

"She had a little accident. Not exactly clear on how it happened."

I'm angry with Mia for putting me in this position. Maybe I should've just minded my own business in the first place.

This sucks big-time.

AUNT PHOEBE MUST have shared her concerns with Uncle Reed because he pays me a visit right before I go to bed.

He sits down in the chair at my desk. "How are things going with you?"

I glance down at my hands. "Fine."

"Things going well at school?"

"Yes, sir."

After a moment, Uncle Reed says, "I know you well enough to see that something's bothering you."

"Uncle Reed, I'm okay. Things are going well for me in my life. I'm getting along with my parents. There's nothing to worry about."

"Are you worried about one of your friends?"

Sometimes I feel like Uncle Reed can see right through to my soul. "Why did you ask me that?"

"Something's troubling you, Divine. I can see it on your face. I'm here if you need my help or just someone to listen."

"Everything's fine, Uncle Reed. I've just had a lot of studying to do. It's not as easy as before. My teachers are losing their minds—giving us all this homework to do. There's drama at school but it's not a big deal."

"Divine, I'm here if you ever need to talk about anything. I want you to know that."

"I know. Aunt Phoebe told me the same thing."

When Uncle Reed leaves the room, I whisper, "I wish I could tell you the truth. I really do."

chapter 11

"*Hey*, Divine."

I turn around to see who's calling my name like they know me. I frown when I see Tim standing there. Folding my arms across my chest, I demand, "What do you want?"

"You seen Mia?"

"No."

"Look, I know we got off on the wrong foot. You don't know me and I think—"

I cut him off. "I'm really in a hurry, Tim." He can't actually believe that I'd want anything to do with him.

"What's up? You think you better than me?"

"Are you doing drugs?" I blurt. "Didn't I just tell you that I'm in a hurry? I have somewhere to be. Why are you trying to make this about you?"

"You don't think I know you acting all funny."

"Why would I be acting funny with you?"

"What has Mia been telling you?"

"She hasn't told me a thing. But since you mentioned it—what do you think she told me?" I don't mention that I know what's up because I don't want Tim going back to Mia and taking it out on her. "Did you know she broke her arm?"

"I didn't do nothing."

"I didn't say you did." He must be feeling guilty. He can say whatever he wants but I'm not stupid. I know he's responsible for what happened.

"Did she tell you that?"

"Mia didn't have to tell me anything. I can see for myself what you're doing to her."

His eyes flash in anger. "You need to keep your eyes on your own man—stay out of my business."

"Tim, why don't you find someone else? You have all these problems with Mia—just leave her alone. If her parents really knew what was going on, her father would shoot you."

"He'll be the one getting shot. I ain't no punk."

"I disagree. Only a punk would go around beating up his girl-friend."

"You don't know what you're talking about."

"Keep your hands off my friend. If you don't . . . you'll be sorry."

He moved closer. "Oh, yeah? What are you gonna do? This ain't Hollywood."

"You better be glad this isn't Hollywood. If it was, my body-guard would have buried your body somewhere beneath the ocean."

Tim laughs. "That's the best you can come up with?"

"No, I'm actually saving it for someone who presents a real

challenge and not some belligerent fool like you. That means 'hostile' in case you don't have a clue. See, I'm not the one. You don't scare me."

"You need to get out of my face."

"You stepped up to me." I switch my backpack to the other shoulder. "Tim, get away from me. I'm so totally bored with the conversation."

"Shut up with your wannabe-white-girl self."

"You can say whatever you want, Tim. Just know that I can give as much as I get. It doesn't bother me because you're nothing more than a wannabe man. News flash . . . a *real* man doesn't hit on girls."

We hold a staring match.

Finally, Tim is the one who looks away.

I step around him and walk to my class. It's obvious to me he's nothing more than a big bully who tries to use intimidation tactics to keep people fearful of him. Tim is nothing more than a joke to me.

I see Mia when I get to third period.

"Your boyfriend's looking for you."

"You talked to him?" she asks me.

"He came up to me asking where you were. I definitely didn't seek him out. I'm surprised he doesn't make you walk around with a tracking device."

"Divine, that's not funny."

"I didn't intend it to be a joke. I was dead serious."

Mia drops down on the bleachers. "I can't take all this drama. It's too much." Tears fill her eyes and roll down her cheeks. "I can't do this anymore. I'm tired of all this fighting."

I sit down beside her. "I'm not trying to fight with you, Mia."

"I'm so stressed-out. Divine, it's like I have to walk around on eggshells. I just want some peace in my life."

"I think that's what we all want, Mia."

"I don't know how all this happened. One minute I was happy with my boyfriend, and then things just went crazy. Now I can't seem to make it all go back to normal. Divine, I just want my life back." She shakes her head. "I'm probably not making any sense."

"Actually, you are. I'd like my life to be as normal as possible. I totally understand."

AUNT PHOEBE HAS Alyssa and me put out the good china on Sunday because Trina and her parents are having dinner with us. The way everything is laid out, you'd think we were expecting royalty to visit.

Mom and Miss Eula came down yesterday and went to church with us. Members of the congregation still get excited whenever mom's present. I guess celebrity never wears off. Last night I overheard my mom saying that Kevin might drive down today.

I'm not real thrilled about it, but Kevin is an okay guy. It looks like he's not going anywhere, so I might as well accept him. At least it doesn't seem like they're rushing into a serious relationship.

I sneak into the kitchen.

Mom and Aunt Phoebe are warming up the food. Miss Eula is at the table putting icing on the red velvet cake.

I stand out of the way, inhaling the delicious aroma of collard greens, baked ham, roasted chicken, candied yams, macaroni and cheese. Mom made the biscuits and a pan of corn bread.

Aunt Phoebe spots me and says, "I didn't know you were in here. Why you standing over in the corner?"

"I wanted to see everything that we're having. I want to make sure I don't miss out on nothing."

"Baby, that's right," Miss Eula says. "Eat as much food as your belly can hold. Lawd knows you need some meat on those bones."

Chance enters the kitchen to retrieve a bottle of water from the fridge. He glances over at me. "What? Why you looking at me like that?"

"I'm just trying to see if you've changed in any way. Or if you've matured."

Chance looks like he's about to respond but suddenly changes his mind when he realizes everybody's watching us.

"Go ahead," I urge. "Say something."

"Leave Chance alone," Mom tells me.

He discreetly gives me the finger.

"That's like so mature, Chance."

Aunt Phoebe glances over her shoulder to where we're standing. "Boy, what you doing over there?"

"Nothing. Just finishing up my water."

"Didn't you go to church with us this morning?" I inquire. "You know what the Bible says about lying."

"Do *you* know what it says?" he counters.

The doorbell sounds and we hear Alyssa talking a few minutes later.

"Our guests are here," Aunt Phoebe announces.

It's only Trina and her family. That's so not a big deal.

Just before dessert, I find myself standing in a puddle of murky-looking water. Twisting my face in a frown, I ask, *What is that?*"

"Trina's water just broke."

"Ugh . . ."

Alyssa takes me by the arm. "Divine, she's going into labor. What are we supposed to do?"

"You're asking me? How would I know?"

"I think I've been in labor all morning," Trina announces. "I thought it was just a bad backache."

Mom walks into the dining room.

"Trina just spilled her water bag all over the floor. Gross."

Mom goes into Mom mode. "Well, the first thing that needs

to be done is getting this floor cleaned. If you two can take care of that, I'll get Chance down here and gather everyone together. Looks like little Joshua's planning to put in an appearance today."

Alyssa pulls me by the hand. "Let's get the mop."

"It's not a two-person job."

"Come with me," Alyssa insists.

"So why do we have to clean up? It's Chance's baby. He should be the one cleaning up the mess."

"Chance should be with Trina. The baby's about to come."

"That baby won't be here for hours. He has plenty of time to mop."

"Divine, it's not the time to be so selfish."

"I can be selfish anytime I want."

Trina's parent leave to go pick up her hospital bag while Chance times her contractions. He's shaking so much that I almost burst out laughing. I control myself because now is not the time when things are so intense.

Trina starts screwing up her face from the pain.

I can't look at her when she's in such agony. Just seeing her like that makes my own stomach hurt.

Miss Eula ambles over with a wet cloth and gently applies it to Trina's forehead. Why, I have no idea. It doesn't look like it's helping to lesson the pain of those contractions.

"They're coming faster," Chance yells.

Mr. and Mrs. Winston arrive and everybody gets ready to go to the hospital. I glance over my shoulder at the red velvet cake. I was really looking forward to sinking my teeth into a slice.

Instead I get to have a front-row seat at the birthing of Trina and Chance's baby boy.

You better be the cutest little baby born, Joshua.

* * *

"CAN YOU CALL Mia for me?" Trina asks. "She wants to be at the hospital when the baby comes. I promised her that I'd call."

I nod.

On the way to the hospital, I call Mia on her cell but get no answer. I try the home number next.

Still no answer.

"Did you talk to her?" Alyssa wants to know.

I shake my head no. "She's probably with Tim."

"What's going on with her?"

"I don't know."

Alyssa's not buying it. "C'mon, Divine. You and Mia have become pretty close. I'm sure she's been confiding in you."

"Just drop it, Alyssa. None of this is your business."

"Then you *do* know something."

"I don't know anything. Why don't you go to Mia and ask her about her business directly?"

"You know she and I don't hang like that."

"Then you don't need to know her business. Just drop it, Alyssa."

"So what are you gonna tell Trina? She's looking for Mia to come to the hospital."

"I'll just have to tell her the truth."

I try Mia's cell one more time. "Why aren't you answering your phone?" I whisper. She must be with Tim and he won't let her— that has to be the reason. She has caller ID, so she knows it's me.

Maybe she's avoiding me.

I leave a message for her at home and on the cell.

We are taken to a family room in the birthing center. I'm so glad to see that it looks more like a living room than a sterile-looking hospital. The bed is covered with nice-looking bedspreads like those at home. "I like this room," I tell Alyssa. "It's a large room, too."

A nurse comes in and prepares the bed for Trina. When it's ready, she helps her settle in.

"It's nice," Trina agrees.

Chance is sitting in a chair beside the bed, holding her hand. He looks like he wants to cry every time one of those contractions rip through her. It's kind of touching to see how much he cares for Trina.

The labor pains seem to taper off and she falls asleep. I glance over at Mom, who explains, "She's only resting. Trina's had quite a workout."

I settle back against the pillows of the sofa against the wall. I slip my headphones on. Might as well pass the time listening to some music while Trina's sleeping.

Chance excuses himself to go to the bathroom. Thankfully, there's one here in the room.

Mr. and Mrs. Winston hold on to each other as they watch over their daughter. Miss Eula's in one corner of the room praying, and Uncle Reed is in the other. Aunt Phoebe and Mom walk out into the hallway. Alyssa's seated in a rocking chair, looking scared to death.

I gesture for her to sit beside me.

"Do you think Trina's okay?" she asks in a low voice.

"I hope so. Everybody looks so scared."

When my mom and Aunt Phoebe walk back into the room, I ask, "Why does everyone look so worried?"

"Having a baby is major," Mom says to me. "Trina is healthy and she's done everything she was supposed to do. I believe she's going to have a healthy delivery. We don't want you and Alyssa to worry. This is normal. Everything she's going through. In a couple of hours, Joshua's going to be here and all this will be a distant memory."

I pray that Mom's right.

chapter 12

Trina's sweating like a pig!

And when those contractions hit, she kind of sounds like one, too. I had to put my hands over my ears for the last one.

"I'm never having a baby," I tell Alyssa as we watch Trina's mom trying to soothe her. "I'm in pain just looking at Trina."

Alyssa agrees. "She's making my stomach hurt."

I walk over to where Mom and Aunt Phoebe are sitting. "Can Alyssa and I go outside? I can't take all this screaming."

"I want you two to stay right inside this room," Aunt Phoebe interjects. "Maybe after you see what it takes to bring a life into this world, you won't be so ready to do it."

"I don't want any children period. I don't need to see this."

"Sugar, just have a seat. Trina's almost dilated nine centimeters. The baby will be born soon."

I gaze at my mom, silently imploring her to step in and tell Aunt Phoebe to shut up. I'm not even talking to her—I was talking to Mom.

After a moment, she betrays me by saying, "I agree with Phoebe. You and Alyssa should be here to witness all that happens during a birth."

As far as I'm concerned, Trina looks like she's about to die. I feel so bad for her—being in all this pain. She keeps talking about pushing, but the nurse tells her to wait.

"I can't do this," she screams.

"Sssh now," Mrs. Winston tells Trina. "It's almost over. It won't be long before this precious little boy is born. C'mon, baby. You can do it."

Trina begins to cry. "I can't do it. I can't . . ."

A doctor and a nurse enter the room and everyone steps away from the bed to allow Trina some privacy while she's being examined. Uncle Reed, Mr. Winston, and Chance step outside.

"You're fully dilated," the doctor announces. "It's time to deliver this little guy."

"What are they doing?" I ask. "I thought they were going to take Trina to the delivery room to have the baby."

"This is a birthing room," Aunt Phoebe explains. "Trina's gonna have the baby in here."

I stand up. "Don't we have to leave?"

"No, family are allowed to stay."

I don't want to stay and watch Joshua being born. Just the mere thought of knowing that much about Trina makes me nauseous. "I don't know if I'll ever be able to eat again," I state. "This is just so gross."

Mom and Aunt Phoebe chuckle.

Alyssa, on the other hand, is trying to see everything. "Divine, I can see the head."

I suddenly feel faint.

"You all right?" Mom asks.

I nod. "I don't think I can handle this, Mom."

"You can just sit over here. You don't have to have a front-row seat for the birthing, hon."

Relieved, I lay my head on the arm of the sofa. This is way too much for me. Despite my not wanting to witness the blessed event, Alyssa feels the need to give me a minute-by-minute description.

Miss Eula and Mrs. Winston are holding Trina up to help her push. She's crying like a baby. Alyssa's dancing around from side to side, trying to see what's going on.

"Divine, the shoulders just came out. Joshua's got a head full of hair."

I nod. It's all I can do to keep from being sick from these smells floating around the room.

"Oh my gosh," Alyssa says. "He's almost out."

Mom and Aunt Phoebe stand up to get a better visual. Why? I don't have a clue.

I would be dying from embarrassment if I were on display like Trina. But with everything that she has going on right now, she probably doesn't care.

Joshua Michael Matthews screams his way into the world at five minutes past five p.m. They lay him on Trina's stomach for a little while before taking him to get cleaned up.

Chance is walking around like he's in a trance.

I get up and touch his arm. "Hey, Daddy. You okay?"

He turns to look at me, his eyes bright with unshed tears. "Did you see him?"

I nod. "He's beautiful. You have a beautiful son."

"What am I gonna do?" he whispers. "Joshua's so little."

"You're going to be a wonderful father," I assure him. "And if you get scared or you don't know what to do, you have Uncle Reed and Mr. Winston. They are great fathers. Just look at you and Trina."

Chance hugs me. "I love you, Divine. Thank you."

"I love you, too." I pull away from him. "Now go check on Joshua."

When I turn around, I find Mom and Aunt Phoebe watching me. "What is it?"

"You were so sweet just now," says Mom. "I'm very proud of you."

"I'm thirsty," I announce. "I'm going down to the cafeteria to get something to drink."

"I'll go with you," Alyssa tells me. "I need a drink myself."

We walk out of Trina's hospital room.

Alyssa loops her arm through mine. "Joshua is so cute," she gushes. "I think he looks just like Trina."

"I think he looks like Chance. He's probably going to keep changing anyway, so by the time he's one year old, he could look like anybody. Look at my little brother. He doesn't look like he did when he was a baby."

"You're right." Alyssa shakes her head. "Girl, that was something, wasn't it? Seeing a baby born like that—I, for sure, don't ever want to be pregnant."

"That's why Aunt Phoebe wanted us to see the birth. She thinks by us seeing it, we won't want to get ourselves in the same position. *It worked*. I can't even look at Trina in the same way again. I know more about her than I ever wanted to know. Talk about gross . . ."

Alyssa laughs. "I feel the same way."

We take the elevator down to the cafeteria. I buy a bottle of water and finish it off before we leave out. Alyssa buys a cookie and a soda, which she devours quickly. We're both anxious to get back upstairs to Trina and the baby.

I try Mia again on her cell.

She answers on the first ring. "I've been trying to call you back. Did Trina have the baby yet?"

"Yeah. Joshua's here. Trina's pretty much out of it."

"I'm on my way there now. I was out with my parents."

"I'll see you when you get here."

Alyssa and I leave the cafeteria. We quickly step out of the path of a team of nurses and doctors rolling a gurney down the hallway toward the elevators.

"Did you see that woman?" I ask. "I heard one of the nurses say she was stabbed like five or six times."

"You lying," Alyssa utters. "I saw a lot of blood but I couldn't tell what happened to her. I did see her face though. She looked like she was in a bad accident."

"I think she was beaten up. Somebody probably tied to rape her or something." I can smell the rancid odor of blood mixed with the antiseptic smell of the hospital, and my stomach starts to feel queasy.

"I feel like I'm going to be sick," I tell Alyssa before running into the nearest restroom.

I barely make it before I spill the contents of my stomach into the first toilet I get to. I vomit until nothing's left.

I wait a few minutes before getting to my feet. I walk over to a nearby sink to rinse out my mouth.

"You okay?" Alyssa questions when I walk out of the rest-room.

I nod. "I hate hospitals." Wrinkling my nose, I add, "I don't like the way they smell."

"While I was out here waiting on you to come out, I heard that

that woman's husband stabbed her. It wasn't a rape like we thought."

"For real?"

Alyssa nods. "Her mother and sister just got here. They said she was planning to leave him."

I immediately think of Mia. "Do they know if she's going to be okay?"

"They just rushed her into surgery."

Just as we're about to pass the hospital chapel, I slow down my pace. "Alyssa, I want to go inside here for a moment. I want to pray for that lady. I think that's horrible what her husband did to her."

"I'll come with you. I'll pray for her, too."

We ease into the chapel as quietly as we can manage. Alyssa's holding on to my arm like it's attached to hers.

We stroll up to the front, noting that only two other people are in the chapel besides us.

"Should we light a candle?" Alyssa asks me, as if I'd know.

"I guess. I don't think it'll hurt."

Alyssa lights two candles—one for each of us.

My eyes closed, I begin to pray silently.

I pray that this woman, a woman I'd never seen before tonight, will make it through surgery and that she'll be able to regain her health and strength and finally leave the man beating her. I also pray for Mia because I don't want her to end up in a hospital or worse—dead.

"We'd better go back up," Alyssa says after we finish praying. "Mama might be getting worried about where we are."

I nod in agreement.

We leave the chapel.

Back upstairs, we walk into Trina's room just as she's trying to get Joshua to breast-feed. Alyssa and I turn around and walk right back out of the room. I've been traumatized enough already—I don't want to see another part of Trina's body. Right now, all I want to do is talk to Madison. He always makes me feel so much better about life.

"I was wondering if you two got lost," Aunt Phoebe says to me when she walks out of Trina's room.

"We stopped at the chapel to pray," I tell her. I don't give out any other details. Aunt Phoebe's real nosy when it comes to me and Alyssa, so I try not to tell her more than she needs to know.

"Mia's on her way here," I tell Trina. "She was out with her parents. That's why she couldn't get here sooner."

Trina nods. "Thanks for calling her."

"No problem."

Uncle Reed and Mr. Winston are nowhere to be found. Mom says it's because Trina was trying to breast-feed.

Noting the grimace on her face at times, I decide if I ever have children, they are going to be bottle-fed. I don't want to have anything to do with even the slightest pain.

WE LEAVE CHANCE and Trina alone with their son to go downstairs.

Aunt Phoebe ushers us out of the hospital room and down the corridor to the elevators. On our way out, we hear this real loud scream. I glance over my shoulder and glimpse the doctor and a nurse trying to calm down a woman on the verge of hysterics.

"That's her," Alyssa tells me. "She's the mother of that lady we saw them bringing in."

Two serious-looking police officers walk past us.

"He killed her," I hear the woman yell to them. "He should be locked away forever. I know he did it. He killed my child."

I stop walking.

"That lady must've died," Alyssa whispers.

Aunt Phoebe eyes me and Alyssa. "Do y'all know them?"

"They brought in this lady who had been beaten and stabbed," I state. "We saw her when we came down earlier to get drinks. There was so much blood."

Tears fill my eyes and run down my face. "I didn't want her to die. Alyssa and I prayed for her in the chapel."

We could still hear the woman yelling at the police officers. "He beat and stabbed her. Why didn't you listen to her? She came to the police for help."

"Hon, I'm so sorry you two had to see something like that." Mom holds me close while Aunt Phoebe comforts Alyssa. "That was so sweet of you both to say a prayer for her. The poor thing . . . she's away from all of that now."

Mom needs to use the restroom before we leave, so we wait near the main entrance of the hospital.

Uncle Reed embraces me, holding me tight as we walk out of the hospital. Aunt Phoebe is walking behind us, probably making sure Alyssa's okay.

A nurse recognizes Mom and asks for her autograph. One autograph leads to another.

A security guard comes over and offers to escort us to our car.

The ride back home is quiet. I'm pretty sure we're all thinking about that dead lady. At least I know that she is heavy on my and Alyssa's minds. It's only now that I realize Mia never showed up at the hospital. She'd said she was on her way when I talked to her.

I consider calling her but change my mind. I'm not in the mood for more of her excuses. She and Trina will have to work out their relationship.

Mom gives me a big hug when we arrive at the house. She and Miss Eula are heading back to Atlanta tonight.

"I love you, baby girl. I'll give you a call later to let you know we made it home."

"I'll be worried if you don't," I tell her.

Inside the house, I feel too numb to do anything. I don't feel like talking to anyone—totally unusual for me. I just stand in the middle of the living room, staring but not really seeing anything.

I can smell the faint hint of Uncle Reed's spicy cologne.

I turn around, facing him. "How can someone who claims to love you be so mean?" I ask. "How could he do that to her? That's not love."

"No, honey, it's not," he responds. "Abuse is about controlling and dominating the other person. Hurting someone is never a sign of love."

"She's dead because she loved him," I mutter.

"Probably so," Aunt Phoebe says. "It's so sad when things like this happen. It just breaks my heart."

"Mine, too," I reply. "Why can this kind of thing happen, Uncle Reed? Why do some men beat their wives like that? I would never let some boy lay a hand on me. Y'all would have to come get me out of jail. I can't go out that way. I don't get why women stay in relationships like this—do they like getting beat up?"

"I don't think that's it at all, sweetheart."

"Then why do they do it?"

"The reasons women stay in abusive relationships are very complicated, Divine. Some women fear the physical harm that might come if they try to leave. Sometimes it's because of love, promises that the abuse will end; sometimes it's guilt. They are being made to believe that the abuse is their fault. Low self-esteem, thinking they can change the person. It can even be financial."

I wipe my eyes with the back of my hand. "How can people just be so mean?"

chapter 13

"*Did* I forget to do something?" I ask when I find both my uncle and aunt at my bedroom door. They don't usually team up unless something is wrong.

I step aside to let them enter.

"No, honey. Your uncle and I just wanted to have a talk with you."

"You're sure I'm not in any trouble? I've had enough drama today and I don't think I can handle anything else right now. If I am, can we wait until tomorrow please?"

Uncle Reed chuckles. "Are you feeling a little guilty about something?"

I shake my head no. "I haven't done anything. Honest."

"Divine, we know that you're burdened about something, and we'd like to help you in any way that we can."

"Uncle Reed," I begin, but he holds up a hand, cutting me off.

"Hear me out please."

"Yes, sir."

"Mia is in trouble, isn't she?" he asks.

I don't respond.

"Is someone hurting her? Your aunt and I have noticed she's been having frequent accidents lately. I've seen the boy she's been running around with, and from what I've heard, he's quick-tempered and quick to fight."

"She's clumsy, I guess."

Aunt Phoebe states, "Divine, I know you don't want anything bad to happen to your friend. But the only way to help Mia is to tell somebody. Are her parents abusing her?"

"No, ma'am," I answer quickly. "Aunt Phoebe . . . Uncle Reed . . . all I can tell you is that her parents wouldn't do something like that."

"Divine, please tell us, what's going on? Who's hitting on Mia? Is it her boyfriend?"

My eyes fill with tears. "I don't want anything to happen to her, but I don't want to be a bad friend either."

"What do you mean, sugar?"

"Aunt Phoebe, I made a promise to her. You don't betray your friends. You and Uncle Reed are always saying that your word is all you really have. How can I go back on my word?"

"There are times when you have to break a vow if it means saving someone's life. Violence and abuse are not situations that should be kept a secret."

"Tim has been hitting Mia," I state. "I've tried to get her to leave him, but she won't. She just makes excuses for him and says that it's all her fault."

"She hasn't said anything to her parents?" Aunt Phoebe questions. "Surely they have to be wondering where all these bruises are coming from."

I shake my head no. "Mia lies about the way she's getting hurt. She hides the bruises on her arms with long-sleeve shirts or sweaters. Now that it's getting warmer, I don't know what's she's going to do."

"Lord have mercy," Aunt Phoebe murmurs.

"I can't stand Tim. He's so mean. He even tried to step up to me, but Madison got up in his face. They almost came to blows."

Uncle Reed's expression changes. "Maybe I need to have a little talk with this boy. You let me know if he puts a hand on you."

"I've taken lots of self-defense classes and I've learned some new moves in my tae kwon do class . . . I wish he would try and get in my face. I'm not afraid of Tim. I don't care if he was in a gang."

"He's been in a gang?" Aunt Phoebe presses a hand to her chest. "There's no telling what this boy has been into. Divine, you stay away from him. Tell Madison to do the same."

"I'm not sure it's true, Aunt Phoebe. That's just what I was told. He had to leave Birmingham and come live with his grandmother because his mother wanted to keep him away from his gangbanging friends."

"Well, just to be safe, I want you to stay away from that boy."

"So what happens now that you know?" I ask.

"I think we should talk to Mia's parents," Uncle Reed suggests. "They need to know what's been going on. If this boy broke her arm, the abuse is escalating."

"She's gonna be so mad at me. Mia's probably not going to be my friend anymore."

"After she has some time to calm down, I believe Mia will understand that you were only trying to help her."

I'm not so sure.

"Before you go to her parents, let me try one more time to get Mia to tell them herself."

Uncle Reed nods. "We'll hold off for now. But, Divine, if she doesn't tell them, we will."

"I understand."

I consider calling Mia after my aunt and uncle leave my room, but chicken out. I keep telling myself that I should wait and tell her face-to-face. Then maybe I can make her understand why I told them.

I did the right thing. I say that over and over to myself, but it doesn't really make me feel any better.

I feel like a horrible friend.

TRINA AND THE baby are home from the hospital today. Chance wanted to stay home from school to help her out, but Uncle Reed doesn't think it's a good idea.

"He's my son. I should be there when he comes home," he fusses on the way to school.

"Trina's mom is gonna be there, Chance. You can go there after school. That's what Daddy was saying."

"I still think I should be there."

"You can always cut class," I tell him.

"And Mama will kill you," Alyssa warns. "I know you want to be with your son, but you do need to finish school."

I see Mia as soon as I step foot on the campus. She waves her one good arm and rushes over to me.

"I'm sorry I didn't get a chance to call you back," Mia says as soon as she catches up with me. "How are Trina and the baby doing? I called her room last night but I didn't get an answer. I can't believe she named that baby Joshua. It's such an old name."

I don't respond.

Mia stops walking and grabs my arm. "Divine, what's wrong? Are you mad at me?"

"No, I'm not mad at you." I release a soft sigh. "There's something I need to tell you, Mia."

"What? Did something happen to Trina?"

I shake my head no. "This has nothing to do with Trina. Last night, while we were at the hospital . . . they brought in this woman—she'd been beaten and stabbed. *By her husband.*"

Mia doesn't respond.

"The woman died. Her husband killed her."

"Did you know her?"

"No. Anyway, I was real upset about it because of how Tim treats you."

"Divine—"

I hold up my hand to stop her. "I'm not done, Mia. I really need you to hear me out on this."

"Okay, so what else happened?"

"My aunt and uncle know about you—they asked me if you were being abused."

Mia looks horrified. "What did you tell them?" She suddenly starts shaking her head in denial. "Please tell me you didn't say anything. Divine, you promised you wouldn't tell a soul. *I trusted you.*"

"What was I supposed to say, Mia? Tim broke your arm."

Mia is furious with me and I can't say it wasn't unexpected. I knew she'd be mad.

"You made a promise, Divine. We're supposed to be girls . . . how could you betray me like that? What kind of friend are you?"

"I'm the kind that cares about you. I don't like what Tim is doing to you. He has no right to put his hands on you."

"I can't believe you!" Mia yells. "Do you have any idea what you did? You've ruined my life."

"I haven't ruined anything. Mia, I'm trying to help you."

"I don't need your help," she snaps. "I never once asked you to help me."

"Oh, really? Then what do you call asking me to come to the hospital when Tim broke your arm? You're being abused."

"Mia," Tim growls, appearing out of nowhere. "What you been telling this tramp?"

Tramp? Did this fool just call *me* a tramp? *Oh, no, he didn't.*

Mia suddenly clamps her lips together. She stands there rolling her eyes at me.

"We were having a private conversation, so could you please leave us alone?" I request.

"You the one who need to be leaving. I need to talk to my girl."

"Divine, see what you started? Why can't you just mind your own business?" Tears roll down Mia's cheeks. "You are *not* my friend. You were never down for me. Just stay away from me from now on. I don't want to talk to you ever again."

Her words sting but I refuse to break down crying. I blink rapidly to keep my tears from falling.

"You heard her," Tim states. "Leave us alone."

"You need to shut up," I tell Tim.

To Mia, I say, "If you don't want to be my friend, I'm okay with that. But you definitely need to get a clue. No boy is worth getting beat up."

Tim glared at his girlfriend. "What you been telling this tramp?"

He really needs to stop calling me a tramp, I fume silently. Before I can open my mouth to tell Tim what I really think of him, he slaps Mia hard, nearly knocking her down to the ground.

"That's for running your mouth. I told you not to be telling my business. I—"

I swing on him without a second thought, connecting with his cheek. "Don't you hit her again," I scream. *"Leave her alone."*

Touching his cheek, Tim growls, "I know you didn't just hit me. Don't no girl put her hands on me."

"But you think it's okay to put your hands on a girl?" Tim and I both ignore Mia, who's sobbing her heart out.

Tim looks like he's about ready to pounce on me, but I'm so ready to take him on. He's messing with the wrong sista now. I'm not going out like Mia.

It's not that I think I can beat Tim, but I'm certainly going to give it my best shot. I reach inside my backpack for something I can use as a weapon.

"Son, I'm about to take you out," I hear someone yell. It takes a moment for it to sink in that it's Madison. "I told you about messing with my girl."

Tim turns around, cussing and taking off his jacket. Madison swings on him. That's my boo. He don't want nobody messing with me.

Alyssa wraps her arms around me. "Are you okay?"

I nod. I glance over at Mia, who is standing there crying her eyes out. I shake my head in disgust. She's upset over Tim—I can't believe her.

Chance and Stephen arrive and pull Tim and Madison apart.

"What's going on here?" Chance demands.

"I was talking to Mia and this jerk walks up and tries to bully me, but I'm not going to just leave her behind with him. She's not his punching bag."

Mia wipes her eyes with a tissue. "Chance, please take Divine away from here. She's messing everything up between me and Tim."

Chance gives me a confused look.

"It's a long story," I tell Chance.

Mia reaches for Tim, but he moves. "Leave me alone. You started this by opening your big mouth."

"Stop yelling at her like that," Chance orders.

Before we can clear out, Mr. McPhearson shows up. "What is the meaning of all this?"

I glance over at Mia. The right side of her face is still a little red where Tim slapped her. Through her tears, she's glaring at me.

"There's nothing going on, Mr. McPhearson," Mia lies.

"If you don't tell the truth right now, my uncle will be over at your house within the next ten or fifteen minutes. This has to stop."

"There is nothing to tell, Divine. Stop trying to make trouble for me and Tim."

"I want all of you in my office now."

"How can you do this to me?" Mia demands.

"I've said all I'm going to say. If you don't tell, I will. It makes no difference to me."

"I'll deny it."

Folding my hands across my chest, I respond, "Doesn't matter. You act like an abused wife. Everybody will be able to see through your lies."

Madison, Chance and I make our way to the principal's office. Tim and Mia are behind us and we can hear them arguing.

"What does she see in him?"

"I have no idea. He's such a major jerk."

A few minutes later, we are all seated in Mr. McPhearson's office with the door closed.

"What is going on, Divine?"

"I think Mia should be the one to tell you."

"I don't have anything to say," she quickly interjects. "Tim and I were minding our own business."

I pull out my cell phone. "I need to call my uncle. Mia is being abused by Tim and she's scared to death to tell anyone. She's mad at me because I've decided not to keep her secret any longer." Pointing to Mia's cast, I say, "He did that. He broke her arm."

"I didn't do nothin'!"

Mr. McPhearson eyes Mia. "Young lady, I need you to tell me the truth."

Her eyes dart to Tim. "I don't have anything to say, sir."

I prepare to dial the number to the church office.

Mia stops me by saying, "Divine, don't do it. Don't call your uncle. I don't want him going to my house and upsetting my mom."

"I assume you're ready to talk then," our principal says.

Mia nods. "Tim and I had a fight and things got a little rough."

"Shut up, tramp."

She flinches at the sound of Tim's voice, which doesn't go unnoticed by Mr. McPhearson. He calls for one of the assistant principals to come to the office.

Tim is escorted to another office, leaving Mia to tell the truth without fear.

"Has Tim been hitting on you?"

Mia drops her head. I can tell she's crying because I see where her tears have stained her shirt. She nods.

I release a sigh of relief.

Mia tells Mr. McPhearson everything. Chance and I are excused and sent to our classes. Mia has to wait on her parents because they were called to come to the school.

"How long have you known about this?" Chance inquires after we leave the office.

"For a few weeks. I made Mia a promise I wouldn't tell, but I just didn't feel good about it. I hated breaking a promise, but I was really scared for her."

"You did the right thing, Divine."

"I've probably lost Mia as a friend though. I betrayed her."

"If she doesn't understand, do you really want her as a friend?"

"I guess not." I give Chance a hug. "Thanks for coming to my rescue. I appreciate it."

"We're family. That's what we do."

ALYSSA CATCHES UP with me at lunchtime. "Hey, I can't believe you hit Tim like that this morning."

"I swung on him because he slapped Mia. I just lost it, Alyssa. He's been hitting her and she's mad at me for telling. I'd rather lose her as a friend than to have Tim kill her."

"I knew something wasn't quite right with those two." Alyssa pauses a moment before asking, "Hey, did he break her arm? I heard she wasn't even at the cheerleading tryouts."

"Yeah. He broke her arm."

"Why didn't you tell me?"

"I couldn't, Alyssa. I promised her I wouldn't. But after we saw that lady at the hospital, I just didn't want Mia to end up like that."

"I see why you got so upset."

"She hates me now."

"Why would you say that?"

"I forced her hand. I told her that if she didn't tell the truth about the abuse, Uncle Reed would be telling her parents. I feel awful."

"C'mon, let's get in line."

"I'm not hungry." I feel myself going into some sort of deep depression. I know I did the right thing, but I'm hurt that Mia doesn't see it that way.

"Mia's parents took her home and Tim's getting kicked out of Temple High. He's caused way too many problems since he's been here."

"That's good," Alyssa says. "He needs to go back to Birmingham."

"I hope he leaves soon. I don't trust him at all."

Tim is on the warpath for sure. I worry that he'll resort to something more deadly.

MOM AND I go visit my little brother, Jason, when I come up to spend the weekend with her. I'm barely in the house when he runs up to me grinning from ear to ear.

"Dee . . ."

"Hey, cutie. You miss me?"

"Miss you."

Laughing, I pick him up. "You're getting so big. I'm not going to be able to carry you around like this much longer."

Jason plants a wet kiss on my cheek. He's such a sweet little boy.

I get down on the floor with Jason. He loves trucks, so Mom and I surprise him with a new one.

Jerome wants me to take some pictures of Jason to send to him. I'm not comfortable with lying, so I say, "Mrs. Campbell . . . Jerome wants me to send him some pictures of Jason. Do you mind if I take some?"

She doesn't respond right away.

I glance over at Mom, hoping she can help me repair the damage.

"Sweetheart, I'm not over my daughter's death, but I have forgiven your father for his part in it. You can send him some pictures."

"I don't want it to upset you. I love my brother and I like coming to visit with you and Jason."

"Nothing is gonna change that, Divine. You can see your brother as much as you want. Lord knows, this boys loves you to death. I hope you two will always be close."

I smile at her. "It's what I want, too."

Mrs. Campbell allows Mom and me to take Jason to Chuck E. Cheese. I don't think I've ever laughed so much, watching him clapping and dancing with the band.

"You really love him," Mom says. "Jason has you wrapped around his little finger."

"I wonder how I'll feel about Ava's baby."

"Probably the same way you feel about Jason. This one will be your little brother or sister, too."

"I'm not crazy about Ava," I confess. "Jerome wants me to be close and all to her, but I can't do it."

"Is it because you think you'd be betraying me?"

"Yes, ma'am."

"Divine, you don't have to worry about me. I'm so over your father. He's very happy with Ava. He loves her and she loves him. I will always hold a special place in my heart for Jerome. Give Ava a chance, hon. You have my blessings."

"How can you be so nice about all this?"

"Because this is what God would have me do. If I want forgiveness, I have to forgive."

Jason falls asleep on the way back home. Mom carries him into the house, placing him in Mrs. Campbell's arms, then we say our good-byes.

"I hope he's not going to be looking for me when he wakes up. I really hate that I don't see him that often."

Mom and I listen to a new gospel CD on the way back across town.

"Is Kevin coming over tonight?" I ask.

"No, he thought you would appreciate some quality time with me."

"We had last night," I say. "Call him and see if he wants to come watch a movie with us."

Mom glances over at me. "You're sure about this?"

I nod. "Seeing as he's not going away anytime soon, I might as well take the time to get to know him. That's what you want, right?"

"Baby girl, I want you to be happy. I want you to feel safe and secure."

"I am. Mom, I want those same things for you."

Mom calls Kevin when we get back to the house. While she's talking to him, I call Madison.

"Hey, baby," he greets me. "What are y'all doing up in Hot-lanta? Wish I was there with you."

"We're getting ready to watch a movie when Kevin gets here. We spent the day with my brother. Madison, you should see him. He's so cute and smart."

"I can't wait to meet the little guy. I can't wait to meet Kevin Nash either."

"I forgot that you two haven't met. Next time he comes to Temple with Mom, I'll bring him to your house."

"Girl, my sisters would lose their minds. I don't know if you wanna do that."

We talk on the phone until Kevin arrives.

"I'll call you later," I tell Madison. "Keep Marcia off the phone."

"Oh, yeah, I knew it was something I had to tell you. She's pregnant."

"Marcia?"

"Yeah. And she's having twins. My parents told her today, she definitely got to find her own place. Marcia say she getting married."

"Wow," I murmur. "You're going to be an uncle."

"Are you excited?"

"I don't know. I think it's too early to tell."

"I'll call you later on tonight."

Mom comes to my room just as I'm ending the call. "You ready?"

"Yes, ma'am."

Arm in arm, we descend the spiral staircase. Kevin is already sitting in the media room by the time we arrive.

"Hello, Kevin."

He awards me a big smile like he's truly happy to see me. "Thank you for inviting me to watch the movie with you and your mom."

"You don't talk at the screen, do you?" I ask. "It's so not cool, but I can't get Mom to stop."

He laughs. "She does get very involved."

"Don't let Divine fool you. She likes to fuss at the characters, too."

"Mom, how you going to put me on blast like that? I'm trying to make a good first impression." I glance over at Kevin. "The other times don't count."

I notice throughout the movie that Mom is constantly watching me. When it ends, I ask, "Is something wrong? You keep staring at me."

"I was just about to ask you the same thing. You look troubled about something, Divine. Hon, do you need to talk?"

"Mom, when you make a promise to someone, you should keep that promise no matter what, right?"

"For the most part, yes, but if breaking that promise means saving a life, I think you should break the vow." Mom pats the empty space beside her. "Come sit here and talk to me."

"I have a friend who is in trouble. She doesn't want anybody to know and she made me promise to keep her secret."

"Is it a bad secret?"

"I think so, but she doesn't. She thinks that she can handle it on her own."

"Can you elaborate a little more?"

I shake my head no. "Mom, I can't. Not right now anyway. I want to give her a chance to straighten this out on her own. If she doesn't, then I'll tell."

"Baby girl, you know you can always come to me or your aunt Phoebe—even your uncle. You can talk to us about anything."

"I know, Mom. It's just that my friend really wants to work this out on her own."

I don't add that Mia is already angry with me for confronting Tim at school. It's only a matter of time before everyone knows, and Mia blames me.

I hope this will spur Mia to end things with Tim once and for all.

chapter 14

I seek out Mia when we return to school on Monday. She's been on my mind all weekend and I'd like to get our friendship back on track.

I have called a couple of times and left messages. I haven't tried any more than that because I'm not chasing her down.

Alyssa and I catch her just before she enters her first-period class. "Hey, Mia," I say. "I was—"

"I don't have nothing to say to you," she tells me, cutting me off midsentence. "You're not my friend, Divine. So don't call me and don't talk to me."

Her voice is filled with so much venom. No, she didn't just say that.

I glance over at my cousin, who's staring at Mia in disbelief.

"What is her problem?" Alyssa wants to know. "I can't believe she treated you like that."

"She's still mad at me for telling your mom and dad that Tim beats her."

"Are you serious?"

I nod. "I told you that she was upset with me. I thought after a couple of days she'd get over it. I guess not." I'm really hurt but trying hard not to show it.

"She was walking around sporting a black eye and she still has a cast on her arm because of Tim. But she's mad at you?"

I nod. *I'm like, so done with her*. It's becoming clear to me that Mia was never the friend that I'd thought she was.

ALYSSA AND I ride with Chance over to the Winston house to visit with Trina and the baby. Chance is a little upset that Mrs. Winston refuses to let him keep Joshua overnight. She keeps saying that he's still too young.

"He's only three weeks old," Alyssa states.

"Joshua is my son. Not hers. It's not like I'ma hurt him. Trina and I took the parenting classes together. And Mama and Daddy are there to help me."

"What's going on between you and Mia?" Trina asks as soon as I walk into her bedroom. "She was coming over until I told her that you'd be here."

I sit down on the edge of her queen-size bed. "What did she tell you?"

Trina continues rocking the baby back and forth, trying to get him to go back to sleep. "She told me that you don't know how to keep your mouth shut. She told me that you can't be trusted and that you're not really my friend."

Those words sting, but I refuse to let the lies my former friend is telling get the best of me. As calmly as I can manage, I respond, "I see Mia's still totally in denial."

"About what? What's going on?"

"Trina, you should ask Mia."

"Since you have such a big mouth, you might as well tell her," Alyssa blurts from the doorway. "If you don't want to, I will. I don't like the way she's treating you when all you tried to do is help the girl."

"Okay, what have I missed?"

"Tim's been hitting on her."

"No way!" Trina exclaims. "Mia wouldn't put up with that."

I don't respond.

Trina's mouth drops open in shock. "Naaah. The Mia I know is definitely not gonna let some boy beat on her. Tim is a jerk, but he ain't crazy enough to hit her. Mia's dad would kill him."

"He didn't know about it," I say. No point in trying to keep it a secret anymore. "Mia's mad at me for telling Aunt Phoebe and Uncle Reed about it. I was supposed to keep it a secret but I couldn't—I was worried about her."

Trina nods in understanding. "I would've done the same thing. I would've told her parents—she knows I'll tell. Especially if she's putting her life in danger."

"Mia doesn't see it that way. I wanted to try and save her, but I don't care anymore. I did what I thought was right. I just wish I'd said something sooner."

Trina shakes her head. "I can't believe she's tripping like that."

I shrug. "It doesn't really matter anymore."

"Well, I'ma have a little talk with Mia. She's wrong and I'ma let her know. She don't need to be going around trying to trash you either. That's not cool."

"You don't have to talk to her, Trina. It's not worth it and I don't want you two mad with each other. Tim caused enough drama. Let's just let it end now."

Chance spends some time cuddling his son before he has to leave for work. Aunt Phoebe is coming to pick us up.

Mia calls Trina while we're there, but she doesn't answer, saying, "I'll give her a call later."

"Don't be mad with her, Trina," I say. "Really, it's okay."

"You sure?"

I nod. "I just want to forget about all this drama. I have a life to live and that's what I intend to do."

Aunt Phoebe shows up shortly after eight to pick us up.

"Where's my little grandbaby?"

Trina brings him out of the newly decorated nursery across from her bedroom. "Here he is."

Aunt Phoebe takes a seat on the leather couch and Trina places Joshua into her open arms.

"I have one thing to say to you girls," Aunt Phoebe states, holding the baby close to her heart. "I've already met one of my grandchildren and I love this little boy dearly, but understand me good—I *can* wait on meeting the rest. Just want to make that clear."

"Why are you telling us that?" I ask. "I'm not doing a thing. I'm a proud member of the big V club."

Frowning, Aunt Phoebe questions, *"The what club?"*

Trina laughs. "She's talking about being a virgin, Mrs. Matthews."

"There's a club now?"

We burst into laughter. Aunt Phoebe is so funny at times. Even when she's not doing it on purpose.

*   *   *

I HAVE SO much homework that the next four days are a blur. It's Friday before I even realize it.

Thankfully, it's a half day. We spend the rest of the afternoon at the mall in Carrollton. Since Mia and I aren't on speaking terms, I seem to run into her everywhere.

She attempts to walk past me and Alyssa as if we're not there, but my cousin isn't about to have that. Alyssa steps right into her path. "You can't speak?"

"Hey."

"Mia, you really need to stop tripping!" Alyssa fusses. "Divine was only trying to help you. She was being a good friend."

Mia glares at me. "You told her those lies. I can't believe you."

"She didn't tell me anything. Divine didn't have to—I saw the bruises on your arms, the black eye—the broken arm . . ."

"They were accidents."

"It was abuse," I counter. "Mia, why don't you try and be honest?"

"Why don't you stay out of my life?"

"You know what, Mia? *I'm out*. I don't need you—I have lots of friends. Friends who truly appreciate me."

"I have friends, too."

"Mia, just shut up! You ought to be grateful that Divine cares for you. You allowed that jerk to hit on you, and now you still lying and trying to cover it up— be for real. Tim was hitting on you and you're still in denial." Alyssa shakes her head in disgust. "Maybe you actually enjoyed getting beat up."

"No, I didn't," Mia snaps. "I didn't like it at all."

It takes her a moment to realize what she said. Mia looks like she's about to cry for a brief second. She takes a deep breath before saying, "Tim has a quick temper and I was getting on his nerves.

He never meant to hurt me. Tim is real jealous because he loves me so much."

"But that's just it. Love is not supposed to hurt, Mia," I tell her. "Tim has no right to put his hands on you for any reason. When he does, that's abuse. If you make him that angry, you two need to just break up. You're not good together."

"Thanks to you, my parents hate him and I'm not allowed to talk to him or see him."

"Mia, that should make you happy," Alyssa points out. "Why do you want to be with someone like that?"

"Because I don't want to be alone. I want somebody to care about me, too."

We all walk over to a nearby bench and sit down.

"Mia, you're a beautiful girl. You don't have to accept the first boy who comes your way. Take your time and really get to know the next one."

"Tim was nice in the beginning. He made me believe that he really cared for me."

"I can't say he didn't care for you, Mia. It's just that he couldn't control his temper. Tim needs anger management."

After our talk, Alyssa and I venture out to the food court to get something to eat while Mia goes in another direction.

"I hope she listens to what we talked about."

I shrug in nonchalance. "I've been telling her the same stuff over and over again. I'm tired of repeating myself. Alyssa, I'm done."

THE NEXT DAY, I wake up early to get all of my chores out of the way. I'm not feeling that great so I just feel like lying around for the rest of the day.

Shortly after eleven a.m., Aunt Phoebe comes to my room, saying, "Sugar, you have a visitor."

"Who is it?" I ask.

"Mia."

"I'm not real sure I want to talk to her. I have a problem with the way she's been treating me." After all, I've been trying to help her and she doesn't appreciate it. Now I have the attitude.

I guess Aunt Phoebe can read minds because she says, "You should go out there and talk to your friend. She's been through something that made her confused, Divine. I believe she's trying to sort it all out. She needs your forgiveness and your support, sugar."

"She really hurt me."

"I know, but remember, Mia was being hurt by someone she thought cared for her. Sugar, she needs a friend."

I'm not ready to be all forgiving. "She should call Trina then."

Aunt Phoebe isn't amused. "Divine, don't do that. Don't turn your back on someone in need."

I rise to my feet. "I'm only doing this for you, Aunt Phoebe."

Mia stands up when I enter the family room. "Divine, hey . . ."

"Do you need something?" I ask.

"I came by to say I'm sorry for the way I've been treating you. I heard what you and Alyssa said to me yesterday at the mall. I'm really sorry about the way I treated you—I was wrong."

"You're right about that," I interject.

In the kitchen a few yards away, Aunt Phoebe clears her throat loudly.

"I accept your apology," I tell Mia. "I was only trying to be a real friend to you. I just thought you deserved better."

"Trina told me she would've done the same thing. She said she would've told my parents after it first happened. Divine, I really thought he cared about me. Tim was so nice at first. He kept telling me that I made him . . . do those things."

"He hit you. Mia, he broke your arm."

"I know." Mia's eyes fill with tears. My dad spent most of last night looking for Tim. He's so mad."

"He's not mad at you. You're his daughter. If that had been me, Jerome would've busted out of prison to get with Tim."

"My mom and dad looked so hurt. They couldn't understand why I didn't come to them. I really thought I could change Tim. I loved him and I just wanted this relationship to work out. He's had such a hard life."

"A lot of people have had hard lives, Mia, and they don't go around abusing other people. I don't get Tim at all, but I do know this. He's a bully and I hope somebody makes him pay for what he did to you."

"He's been calling my cell phone all day. My dad answered a couple of times but Tim just hung up. Mom's getting the number changed."

"I think that's a good idea."

"My parents are planning to press charges against Tim. Divine, I don't want him in jail."

I look at her like she's lost her mind. What is Mia thinking? "Why not? He's going to end up there one day anyway. Why not now?"

"I still care about him—even if we're not together."

"How can you have feelings for a boy who hurt you?"

"I don't know." Wiping her eyes, Mia says, "Divine, I don't want to be with him anymore, but my feelings haven't gone away."

"Mia, you're going to find a nice guy one day soon. Please don't let Tim apologize his way back into your life. I'm so glad you told your parents the truth."

"I just hate seeing the look of disappointment on their faces. I don't think they'll ever trust me again."

"They will," I tell Mia. "It may take some time but they'll trust you again. Parents are like that."

Playing with the strap of her purse, Mia says, "They're hurt and it's all my fault—all of this is my fault."

"This is Tim's fault, Mia. *Not yours*. Don't you forget that—okay?"

She gives a slight nod.

Mia stands up. "I promised my mom that I wouldn't be gone long. I'd better get going."

Her cell phone rings.

"It's Tim," she announces with a sigh. "I really wish he'd stop calling me."

"Aren't you about to get the number changed?"

Mia nods. "Yeah. Mom and I are going to the Sprint store when I get back home."

"Why don't you just turn it off for now? Tim's just going to keep calling you. If the phone's off, the call will go straight to voice mail."

"That'll take care of the phone, but what if I run into him? I think he's watching my house."

"Don't worry about that. I'll ask Aunt Phoebe to give you a ride home. She won't mind."

"You're sure?"

I nod.

"Aunt Phoebe, would you give Mia a ride home?" I ask. "She's afraid that Tim might be somewhere waiting on her."

"Sugar, just give me a minute. I'll make sure you get home safe."

"Thank you."

"My aunt keeps a bat in the van. She'll beat Tim down if she has to," I tell Mia.

"I'll call my mom and let her know your aunt's driving me home."

Ten minutes later, we climb into the van. Aunt Phoebe drops Mia off safely. Her parents come out to talk with Aunt Phoebe for a few minutes.

Back at home, Aunt Phoebe says, "I'm so glad that girl told her parents about the abuse."

"Me, too. Her dad sounds like he's ready to kill Tim on sight. If he has any brains, Tim better stay out of the way."

chapter 15

The following week drags by at a snail's pace. Alyssa and I fight through mountains of homework and studying for tests in math and science while taking time out for choir rehearsal on Wednesday night. This week Uncle Reed postpones our family game night until Saturday because we have so much schoolwork to do.

By Friday, I'm ready to become a high school dropout, I'm so tired of my classes, but the moment passes and I envision myself standing on a corner begging for money.

It's definitely not the life I want for myself.

I notice the flashing red light when I go through my backpack looking for a pen and take a chance to check my phone. Rhyann texts me while I'm in my fifth-period class.

Can u believe this jerk is cheating on me? I'm so thru with him.
Call me or text me back. I'm so upset, I have 2 leave school early.
I need u, so don't 4get to call me.

Total drama. Thank God it's Friday.

Like I really need more of that in my life. I locate my pen and close up my backpack.

I'm having a hard time staying attentive to the boring substitute teacher we have in math. She talks in this low monotone and it's lulling me to sleep. If the bell doesn't ring soon, I'm going to need toothpicks just to keep my eyes open.

Freedom comes at two-twenty when the bell rings.

I see Mia after class and wait for her to catch up with me.

"Have you seen Tim today?" she asks.

"No. Why?" I notice she keeps looking around, scanning our surroundings. "Have you seen him?"

"I thought I did but I couldn't be sure. My parents think that he's the person who keeps calling the house and hanging up."

"I wouldn't be surprised. He's crazy."

"I wish I'd never met him, Divine. He's making my life miserable. I thought he really cared about me because he kept saying that I was the best girlfriend he's ever had and that he never loved anybody like he loves me. Divine, now I feel like he's stalking me. I don't think he's gonna just walk away—he's really beginning to scare me. The last time I told him that we should break up, he talked about killing himself. He really tripped out on me."

"You can't let him do that to you because, if you do, then Tim's still winning. Your parents know the truth about him now. They're not going to let him hurt you. And you know we got your back here at school."

"I just really wish I'd never met him. You know?"

"But you did, Mia. You can't go back and rewrite history."

Sighing loudly, she nods. "You're right."

"Mia, you just have to learn from your past and look toward your future. That's what Aunt Phoebe always tells me."

Mia changes the subject when she says, "I went to Trina's house last night. Joshua's so cute." Breaking into a smile, she adds, "She let me hold him. I don't think her mom was thrilled about that. She's real bossy when it comes to that baby. Trina told me that Chance is having a real problem with her parents about Joshua."

I don't comment. I'm not trying to tell my cousin's business. But it is true. Chance feels like Mr. and Mrs. Winston don't want him involved with Joshua. They won't even let him bring the baby over to our house. They keep saying he's still too new. Aunt Phoebe says she's going to wait a little while longer before having a word with them. Joshua is her grandson, too, and she intends to be a part of his life.

"Tim wanted me to have a baby for him."

Mia's words stop me dead in my tracks. *Say what?*

She repeats her statement. "He said it would bring us closer together."

I shake my head in puzzlement. "He really is a psycho."

"Tim was so angry when I told him that I wasn't ready to be a mom. He kept saying that I thought I was too good to have his baby. He kept saying he was gonna get me pregnant anyway."

"Mia, are you pregnant?"

She shakes her head no. "I'm not. Thank God."

"I'm glad you're not going to have a baby, but Mia—Tim could've given you a disease. Have you gotten checked out by a doctor? I'm talking about getting an HIV test."

Mia shakes her head. "I'm scared."

"You have to get tested," I urge. "For all you know, Tim could've been cheating on you."

"I don't want my mama to find out about me and Tim . . . you know. My parents don't have any idea that I've had sex. At least I don't think they know."

"Mia, your parents love you. I'm not one for trying to have grown-ups all in my business, but when it comes to something like this, I really think you need to talk to your mom."

Shaking her head, Mia refuses. "Divine, you don't know my mother. She'll think I'm a tramp or something. She's always talking about fast girls, calling them tramps."

"No, she won't. Your mother knows you better than anybody else. She's not going to think that you're a bad person because you lost your virginity."

Mia's eyes tear up. "It's not like I really wanted to do it. Tim . . . he just kept pressuring me and he'd get so mad. I just didn't want to fight with him."

"He's mean," I say.

"I just wanted a nice boyfriend. All I seem to meet are a bunch of jerks. You came here from California and met Madison. I've been here my entire life and I haven't met one guy that really cared about me."

"You'll meet someone. But first, you need to heal from all you've been through with Tim. And, Mia . . . don't ever let another guy pressure you into something you really don't want to do. My mom told me that if you say no . . . *no means no*. And that it's rape if a guy doesn't listen."

Mia wipes her eyes. "I'm so stupid."

I embrace her. "Stop being so hard on yourself. It's over, Mia. Now it's time for you to try and move on with your life."

"How can I? I have to get tested for HIV . . . I'm scared to death that Tim's going to jump out of the bushes someday and attack me . . . Divine, I'm so scared all the time."

I suddenly feel this urge to pray for Mia.

"I don't want you tripping or nothing, but God just placed it on my heart to pray for you. This has never happened before in my entire life, but I know I need to do it. I hope you don't think I'm a freak or something."

"I wanna pray," Mia says to me.

Her sixth-period class is right beside mine, so I'm not worried about being late. We find a vacant corner and close our eyes. I say a quick prayer for protection over Mia.

"Thanks so much for being my friend, Divine," Mia says when I finish. "I've been so mean to you and I'm sorry."

"We're cool. It's all good."

"Oh, I called my mom and she said it was okay for me to go home with you today. I'll meet you right here if that's fine with you?"

"Great. We'd better get in class. The tardy bell is about to ring."

I step inside my class just as it goes off.

My teacher gives me a sidelong glance. "You're supposed to be in your seat by the time the tardy bell rings, Miss Matthews-Hardison."

"Yes, sir." I quickly take my seat. "Sorry about that."

Mia and I meet Alyssa after school by the library.

"You're coming to our house?" Alyssa asks.

"Yeah. Me and Divine need to work on our health project together.

"I'm so glad you're my partner," Mia tells me. "I had Callie Malcolm last time and she didn't do a thing. I ended up having to do the entire project by myself. I was so mad."

"I hope she got an F for her grade."

Mia shakes her head. "Nope. She got the same grade I did. That's why I was so mad. I was ready to get with her."

The minute we step off the campus, Tim suddenly appears in our path. "I need to talk to you, Mia."

She stops in her tracks. "I have nothing to say to you, Tim. Just go away."

"I ain't going nowhere. We need to talk."

"About what?" she demands.

Before he can respond, Nicholas joins us, saying, "Y'all ready to walk home? I'm sorry I held you up."

"Yeah, we're ready to go," I respond. "And we'll call the police if Tim don't leave us alone."

"Shut up, tramp," Tim yells. "You talk too much." He then cusses at me.

I'm tempted to give as much as I'm getting, but because I'm trying to live right, I don't. Instead, I ignore him while pulling out my cell phone. I intend to keep it handy in the event we need to call the police. I notice Alyssa already has her phone in her hand.

"We need to get home," she states.

"Mia, you ain't going nowhere. Not till I'm done talking to you. We need to get some things straight."

This boy is seriously bugging!

"Mia doesn't want to talk to you, Tim. Why don't you just leave her alone?" Nicholas tells him.

"Who you s'pposed to be? *Her man now?*"

Nicholas isn't about to back down. "We don't have to explain anything to you. Why don't you just leave Mia alone? She's made it clear that she doesn't want to be bothered with you."

Tim swings on Nicholas, who blocks it successfully.

Alyssa grabs Mia by the hand, pulling her out of the way.

Nicholas moves into a fighting stance.

I move into position because I'm not about to let him have all the fun. I'm tired of being called a tramp among other names by this punk.

Tim laughs. "Oh, I see . . . y'all think you know some karate?"

Nicholas and I glance at each other and chuckle.

Tim swings a second time. Nicholas successfully deflects the blow by bringing his left hand from the left to the right.

One of the teachers comes running over. He and Tim have words until Mr. Henderson threatens to call the police.

Tim walks away, leaving a string of profanity behind. I breathe a sigh of relief.

"Kam sa hamnida," I say to Nicholas. In English it means "thank you."

"Cheon ma ne yo," he responds, which means "you're welcome."

I look over my shoulder at Mia and Alyssa. Mia's crying her eyes out while my cousin tries to console her.

"He's not gonna leave me alone."

"Call your dad and tell him what just happened," I encourage. "I'm sure they can get a restraining order or something to keep Tim away from you."

By the time we get to the house, Mia has calmed down. I'm so grateful that Nicholas was there. It probably would've taken me and him both to take down Tim. I silently consider bringing a bat to school with me for protection.

Mia tells her father what happened. When she gets off the phone, she tells us, "My parents said I'm not gonna be walking home no more. Not until Tim is back in Birmingham. They are driving me to school and picking me up. We're also getting a restraining order."

I get another text message from Rhyann. I send her a reply to let her know that I'll be calling her later in the evening. Right now, I can only deal with one crisis at a time.

Mia and I settle in my bedroom and prepare to work on our project. We have to do a brochure and create an ad to promote awareness of sexually transmitted diseases. Talk about bad timing. Mia's already dealing with a lot, and now she's trying to summon up courage to have a medical checkup and tests for STDs. Seeing the stuff my friends are going through, I'm not interested in traveling down that same road.

We work until Aunt Phoebe calls us for dinner.

After a plate of meat loaf, mashed potatoes, and gravy, the last thing I want to do is homework. I'm ready for a nap and can't seem to stop yawning.

"You and Madison must have stayed up late talking on the phone," Mia says.

I nod. "He worked until eleven, so I didn't get a chance to talk to him until sometime after midnight. My boo is trying to make him some money. He wants to buy a car."

"That's so nice. That's all I want. A normal relationship."

I glance over at her. "You'll get that, Mia. I think we all have to go through some crazy relationships at one time or another. Not sure why. Maybe it's supposed to build character or something."

"Then I must have a lot of character after what I've been through. The truth is that I'm really not in any hurry. I need to re-cover from my recent drama."

I work on the research portion of our project while Mia handles the creative part. She wants to be a graphic artist one day.

We don't complete our project until shortly after eight.

After Mia's parents pick her up, I shower and get ready for bed.

My cell rings and it's Rhyann.

"I thought you were going to call me."

"Mia and I had a project to work on. She just left not too long ago."

"Can you talk now?"

I'm so sleepy, but I can tell Rhyann's upset. "Yeah. I can talk. Tell me what happened."

"Carson's cheating on me. *Me*."

"How did you find out?"

"He sent me an instant message that was meant for her. Can you believe that? Girl, my brothers are ready to hang him high."

"Well, maybe because his relationship with you is so new, Carson's not real serious right now."

"Then he should tell me. I was up-front about being a one-man woman. That fool was just trying to play me. He thought he was going to get me to do the between-the-sheets tango. Humph. I'm a queen. You can't just walk up and take the throne—you have to be born with royal blood flowing through your veins. I'm not giving my royalty to just anybody."

Rhyann makes me laugh sometimes with the stuff she says. She's clearly upset right now, so I restrain myself from cracking up.

"Have you talked to Carson?"

"I told him about himself. He tried to deny it, but you know I save everything. Then he said he was just playing around on the internet. Claimed he'd met her in a chat room. I really don't give a flip where he met her. Cheating is cheating."

"I totally agree."

"I really liked him," Rhyann whines. "He was my boo."

Rhyann doesn't have a thing to worry about. She attracts guys like a magnet.

"I told him he was out of my life for good. I don't need to be disrespected. It's his loss. Not mine."

Rhyann continues ranting. I'm amazed she's able to catch her breath, she's talking so fast.

"Hey, I'm smart. I'm cute and I have a nice body. There's nothing wrong with me . . ."

My eyelids grow heavy. All I want to do is sleep right about now.

"Dee . . . are you there?"

"Huh? Yeah. I'm here." I must have fallen asleep on Rhyann. I try to cut into her monologue. "I'll call you tomorrow. I'm tired and it's getting late."

Rhyann continues talking as if I hadn't said anything. "Dee, I deserve so much better than this."

"Yeah. You do," I mumble.

"I know what I need to do. I need to find that hoochie and beat her down. That's what I need to do. Out there messing with my man."

"Why would you want to fight her? She may not know she's the other woman. Rhyann, for all you know, you could be the other woman." I stifle my yawn.

"I'll never settle for being the other woman. I'm too fine for that."

And people think I'm conceited. They haven't met Rhyann—she's full of confidence. No self-esteem issues there.

Rhyann sighs in resignation. "I'll get past this heartache. I always do."

I try one more time. "Rhyann, I have to get off the phone."

"Oh. Okay. Well, thanks for being here for me. I appreciate it. You always down for me."

"I'll give you a call tomorrow."

Without waiting for a response, I end the call. The last thing I remember about this night is putting my cell phone on the bedside table.

ALYSSA AND I meet up with Stacy over at Penny's house on Saturday afternoon. We're planning to watch a chick flick and devour pizza, chips, and soda.

"I heard you and Nicholas were about to kick some tail yesterday," Stacy says.

"He probably would've smashed both of us into the ground, but we were going to give it our best shot," I respond with a laugh.

"I was scared he was gonna pull out a gun or something," Alyssa confesses.

A thread of fear runs down my spine. "You think he carries a gun?"

"I don't know, but I wouldn't be surprised."

"Hey, Divine," Penny begins. "What's up with your friends in Los Angeles? You talk to them lately?"

"I talk to Rhyann and Mimi on a regular basis. They're doing okay. Mimi's in love again and Rhyann's ready to fight some girl who's been cheating with her boyfriend. I told her it's whack to want to beat up the girl. It's the boyfriend who was cheating. She needs to just dump him and move on."

Alyssa picks up a slice of pizza. "Rhyann's so pretty. She can get any guy she wants."

"I'm not wasting my time with dogs anymore," Stacy declares. "I'm gonna focus on my studies so I can go to college, get me a degree, and make lots of dollars. The men will come when I'm driving around in my Lexus."

Her cell phone starts blaring a Jay-Z ringtone.

She checks the caller ID, then squeals, "This is him. It's Eric. Y'all, I gotta take this." Stacy runs out of the room in search of some privacy.

"Eric? Who's that?" I inquire. I thought she was talking to Anthony. That's who took her to the Valentine's Day Dance.

Penny and Alyssa are just as puzzled as I am.

"When did she and Anthony break up?" Penny asks.

As if we have any idea of what's going on with Stacy. "I have no idea. I don't have a clue what's going on," I answer.

Alyssa shrugs, but Penny says, "I don't think they were going together. They were just talking and they went to the dance together."

"They sure looked like they were together," I state. "They were always hugging at school and kissing."

"Friends with benefits," Alyssa murmurs with a chuckle. "That's the new trend."

"It might be the new trend, and, you know, I'm one for setting my own trends—that's not one I'm interested in." I reach for a second slice of pizza, putting it on my plate.

"I like having a boyfriend. Call me old-fashioned." Alyssa takes a long sip of her soda.

After fifteen minutes pass, Penny calls out to Stacy, "C'mon. We're ready to watch the movie. Tell him you'll call him back."

"I'll be there in five minutes," she yells back.

Another fifteen minutes pass.

"Are we gonna watch the movie or not?" Alyssa questions.

"We're starting the movie, Stacy."

No response.

Halfway through the movie, Stacy joins us, grinning from ear to ear. "Sorry, y'all, but I really needed to talk to him. He's so cute and—"

"Ssssssh," we utter in unison. We're deliberately ignoring Stacy. We have this unspoken rule that no boy is supposed to intrude on our girl time. Madison has called me twice already, but I'm not rushing off to talk to him.

Why can't more people be like me?

When the movie ends, Stacy starts up again. "When y'all meet Eric, you'll understand. He's gorgeous."

"I thought you were taking a sabbatical from boys," I say.

"A what?"

"Sabbatical," I repeat. "It means an extended period of leave or rest. Anyway, where did you meet this Eric person? I hope not on the internet."

"I didn't meet him on the internet. We met at the band competition. He plays in the band at Carrollton High. I'm not rushing into anything, but he's just so nice and he says all the right things."

"Then why were you swearing off men before Eric called?" Penny questions. "What happened with you and Anthony?"

"Anthony was only interested in my body. He's looking for sex—not a girlfriend."

"That seems to be going around," Penny mutters. "Must be contagious. I wonder how boys would feel if we treated them like that?"

"Euphoric," I respond.

Frowning, Stacy says, "If that means they'd be happy—that's it exactly."

chapter 16

Mia comes over to the house shortly after we arrive home from church. We go to my bedroom and talk.

"Girl, you got some skills. I like those moves you and Nicholas were doing. I wish I could do something like that. Tim looked like he didn't know what to do."

"Why don't you take classes with me?" I suggest. "The more I think of it, the more I believe it's a great idea."

Shaking her head, Mia says, "We can't afford it. My dad hasn't found another job yet. You know he got laid off back in October, and my mom only works part-time."

"I hope your dad can find another job soon."

"Me, too. He's been looking every day. He thinks he's gonna have to drive back and forth to Atlanta. My dad hates that, but if that's what he has to do, he'll do it. Daddy's a real hard worker. He doesn't want my mom to work. He likes her being at home."

Alyssa knocks on my bedroom door.

"Come in."

"Is this a private conversation or can I join in?" she asks.

"Sure," I tell Alyssa.

"What's going on, Mia?" she greets.

"Nothing much. Just sitting here talking with Divine. I really wish I could meet someone like Stephen or Madison. You guys are so lucky."

"You *will* find someone nice," I assure Mia. "Like I told you before, you need to take some time to get over everything that Tim put you through. You might have . . . what's it called? Traumatic stress syndrome."

Alyssa laughs. "And when did you get your medical degree?"

"I'm serious. All that drama with Tim might scar Mia for life."

"I don't feel scarred. I just feel angry. I'm so mad at myself for being so stupid. I'm mad at myself for being scared of a punk like that." A tear rolls down Mia's cheek. "I hate that every time I see him, he scares me."

Mia's mom comes to pick her up after dinner. Mia gives me a hug when I walk her to the door. "Thanks for being my friend. I don't know what I'd do without you."

"Same here," I respond.

"How's she doing?" Aunt Phoebe asks me when I walk into the kitchen. She's washing dishes, so I pick up a towel to help her out. I much prefer drying than actually sticking my hands into a sink of greasy water.

"I guess Mia's okay. She's really beating herself up though. She feels stupid for allowing things to go the way they did with Tim. I keep telling her that she's not stupid, but Aunt Phoebe, I have to be honest—I felt the same way about her. I thought she was pretty stupid for letting him hit on her like that."

"I can't say that I fully understand why she continued her relationship with that boy, but when emotions get all tangled up or you feel like that person is your only tie to happiness—you stay. Or you don't leave because you're just too scared. Sugar, don't you be so hard on Mia. Unless you walk in her shoes, you may not ever fully understand."

"I feel like such a hypocrite. I was *really* stupid when I was talking to Theopolis Mack. The only difference is that Mia knew her attacker. I had no clue who I was talking to over the internet."

"You need to take your own advice, Divine. Don't dwell on mistakes of the past. Learn from them and move on toward your future."

I nod in understanding.

Aunt Phoebe and I get the kitchen cleaned in no time. She works much faster than Alyssa.

"I see Madison's working at McDonald's," she says. "I saw him in his uniform when I was on my way to the supermarket today."

"He wants a car but his parents say he has to raise half the money for it."

"I agree. I think that's more than fair."

I chuckle. "That's not a major surprise, Aunt Phoebe. You're a parent and that's how you're wired to work."

"You make me sound like a machine."

"I don't mean it quite like that." Putting away the last glass, I add, "It's just that when you become a grown-up, I guess your whole brain starts working in a different way."

"It's called maturity."

"Or old age," I tease.

Aunt Phoebe places her hands on her hips. "I know good and well you didn't just accuse me of being old."

"It's not like you're in your twenties or even your thirties anymore."

Taking me by the hand, Aunt Phoebe leads me into the family room. We sit side by side on the sofa.

Alyssa walks in. "Oh! Am I interrupting?"

"No," Aunt Phoebe responds. "You're just in time. I'm about to school your cousin here on what getting older or, more specifically, being in your forties means."

"I need to sit down for this," Alyssa replies.

"So what does being forty mean?" I ask.

"It means freedom," Aunt Phoebe says.

Alyssa and I exchange puzzled looks. What in the world is Aunt Phoebe talking about? I wonder.

"Turning forty releases you from a lot of the stuff that has held you hostage for years."

"Like what?" Alyssa asks.

"Like being a slave to worrying about what others think about you. You wake up one day and you just don't care. It's all about you and how you feel about yourself."

"Divine's already there," Alyssa replies with a laugh.

I pinch her on the arm in response.

"I used to get so caught up in how others viewed me. I wanted to dress to impress—"

I cut Aunt Phoebe off when I blurt, "When?"

"Oh, sugar, I used to be a slave to fashion. I wouldn't buy anything that didn't have somebody's name on it."

"What's wrong with that?"

"Nothing's wrong with it, but you shouldn't let clothing define who you are. Some people think that if you wear designer clothes, drive a luxury car, or live in a huge house, it makes you look successful. Makes you feel as if you're worthy . . . People are lulled into buying things they can ill afford, and when the debts mount and threaten to overtake them, it's too much to bear. At some point in life, it's important to understand that you are the same person in designer rags that you are in cheap threads. I found that freedom in turning forty."

"I get that, Aunt Phoebe. But what I don't understand is why you had to totally go the other way."

She frowns. "What are you talking about?"

"You turned against fashion. How could you do that?"

"I didn't turn against it. Divine, I just refuse to . . . sugar, there was a time when I owned at least twenty or so credit cards. And I used them. Boy, did I use them. Reed and I were in so much debt. It wasn't because of him or that he wasn't making money. It was me. I was the first lady. I felt I had to look a certain way and act a certain way. I wanted to be sophisticated and elegant. Like the first ladies I saw in Atlanta."

"Mama, what happened?" Alyssa asks before I can get the same question out of my mouth.

"Well, here I was in debt to my eyeballs but dressed to the nines, and those ol' snooty women still didn't care one whit about me. I was still an outsider. I don't know if you remember this, Alyssa, because you were so young, but I went out and got a job. I worked until I paid off all those credit cards, and then I got rid of them. For a long time I felt like a failure. But when I celebrated my fortieth birthday—the lightbulb came on. I was free."

"And you stopped keeping up with fashion and style, huh?" I shake my head. "If that's what happens when you turn forty, I don't want none of it. Aunt Phoebe, I hope you warned Mom."

She laughs. "Your mother has always known who she is. I was the one searching for an identity."

"So who are you, Aunt Phoebe?"

"I am me," she replies with a laugh. "I am a woman who loves. I love God. I love my family. I love life and I love myself. I may not be the most fashionable and I may not drive a luxury car—I could if I wanted to. Reed and I don't have any credit card debt. If we can't pay it off at the end of the month, we don't buy it. We love our life because we're not held hostage by a mountain of debt."

I'm rich so I won't ever have to worry about bills and stuff. My mom makes over $30 million a year. I'll never run out of money because she puts half of it in a trust for me. She wants to make sure I never have to want for anything.

Aunt Phoebe looks at me and says, "I hope you'll never have to worry about money, but if you don't use wisdom, that money will be gone before you know it."

"I hear you, Aunt Phoebe. Still, why can't you still maintain good fashion sense, even if it doesn't have a designer label? I'm not getting that. You like to wear those big hats with bows and feathers. Why do you have to wear one with every outfit?"

"Sugar, dressing up for God is a part of our heritage. It's our way of presenting the best of ourselves to the Lord. During slavery, women had two dresses if they were lucky. One for everyday and a good one for Sunday. When slavery ended, a lot of them found jobs in domestic service and had to wear uniforms. Sunday was the only time they could express their creativity, so to speak. It was a statement of freedom."

"Wow," I murmur. "I'd dress up, too, if I'd had to go through that."

"The Bible speaks on the importance of women covering their heads. So, it's not just about fashion."

"So when you wear all those bright-colored suits with the matching big hats, you're just expressing your own style and worshipping God?"

Aunt Phoebe nods. "You can say that I'm embracing my individuality and my heritage. I love feathers, flowers, and bows, and I love hats."

"Does it matter what you wear to church?" I ask.

"Sugar, what matters is that you attend church. Hats have always been a part of my attire. My mother wore hats, and as children we were taught that you're not really dressed up unless you had on a hat and gloves."

"I still have the hats Mama bought me to wear on Easter," Alyssa states. "I used to love my hats, but then when I saw that none of the other girls at church were wearing them, I stopped wearing mine."

"I like hats," I say. "But not like the ones you wear, Aunt Phoebe."

"You don't have to wear big ones like mine," Aunt Phoebe tells me. "It's about freedom of expression."

"I can get with that," I respond. "I'm all about setting my own trends."

"Mama, now when I see you in your bright-colored suits and hats, I'm gonna be thinking about all those women who had to wear uniforms and the slaves who only had two dresses."

I agree. "Aunt Phoebe, I'm not going to tease you about your hats anymore. Keep wearing them with pride."

"It's called hatitude," Aunt Phoebe responds with a chuckle.

"Aunt Phoebe, don't say that to anybody else." Alyssa and I both laugh. "That's so not cute."

LATER ON THAT evening, Aunt Phoebe comes to my room to tell me that my dad's on the phone. He tries to call me twice a month. He has to call collect, so he tries to be respectful of my aunt and uncle's finances. Mom offered to reimburse them for the charges, but Uncle Reed turned down her offer.

I take the phone out of Aunt Phoebe's hand. "Hello, Jerome."

"How you doing, baby girl?"

"I'm doing okay. How are you?"

"Taking it one day at a time. Nothing more I can do. When was the last time you saw Jason?"

"Not too long ago. I sent you some pictures of him. He's getting so big and he's talking more."

"Do you have any more pictures of him?"

"I sent you the ones from his birthday party, right? I don't have any more. I told Mrs. Campbell the truth, Jerome. She's been so nice to me and I just didn't want to lie to her."

"What did she say?"

"Not a whole lot, but she did give me permission to take the pictures. She's still grieving and it's going to take time. She did say she forgives you."

"I'm glad to hear that. I wasn't sure she would ever forgive me, but I'd like to talk to her one day. I've thought about writing to her and telling her that I never meant to hurt Shelly, but I don't want to upset her. I hope and pray that I'll be able to see my son in person. I want him to get to know me."

I'm not real sure that's ever going to happen, but I don't tell Jerome that because I don't want to depress him. She's never said it, but I have a feeling that Mrs. Campbell is never going to let him near Jason.

"You talk to Ava yet? I told her you would be calling. She's eager to hear from you."

I decide to be totally honest with my dad. "Jerome, I don't really know what to say to her. I know she's your wife now, but—"

"She's your stepmother," he interjects, as if that's going to make a difference to me. Ava is the stepwitch as far as I'm concerned. Mom says I should give Ava a chance, but I still feel like I'd be betraying her in some way.

"Baby girl, I want you to get to know Ava. She's a good woman and she loves me, in spite of everything I did in the past. She never stopped loving me."

"I'm happy for you, Jerome. I really am, but you can't just expect me to forget everything that's happened with her. She was so mean to my mom. I'm not tripping though. It's just going to take time, you know?"

"I understand what you saying. Your mama and I got divorced, but I'm still your daddy. I don't want you to forget that, Divine. No matter what, I'll always be your daddy. When Ava gives birth, you're gonna have a little sister or another brother. I need you to be there for her. Just like you are for Jason. There was a time that you didn't even want to get to know him. Remember? Now you love him to death."

"His mom is dead," I state. "I don't have to deal with drama."

"Ava's not gonna give you drama. Why do you think that she would? Look, that stuff that went down with her and your mama, it's all over. Ava knows that it was wrong and she regrets it. She was acting out of her love for me. Can't you see that?"

Like that's a good excuse.

I'm tired of hearing about Ava and her needs so I ask, "Jerome, can we please talk about something else?"

"Sure. What do you want to talk about?"

"Have you heard when you might be getting out?"

"Not yet. I know one thing—this is not something I ever want to repeat. I hate being in here. How's school?"

"Okay. It's school. Oh, I got my blue belt in tae kwon do." Jerome is a black belt in tae kwon do and the reason I started studying in the first place.

"Congratulations. I'm so proud of you, baby girl. You know I didn't think you were gonna stick with it."

"I didn't either. But once I started the class and got my yellow belt, I wanted to continue studying. Now I love it. I'm competing in an upcoming competition in the sparring division."

"I wish I could be there to cheer you on."

"I know you'll be there in spirit."

Jerome's time is up. "I gotta go but you should be getting a letter from me by the end of the week."

When I walk into her room, Alyssa asks, "How's Uncle Jerome doing?"

"He's okay. Just bugging me about Ava. He wants me to get to know her better." As if.

Alyssa turns away from her computer. "She seems like she's an okay person."

I drop down to the huge floor pillow, making myself comfortable. "She doesn't like my mom."

"I don't think Aunt Kara really cares for her either."

"If she can't stand Mom, she's not going to like me much."

"You can't really say that, Divine. You are Uncle Jerome's daughter. She's not gonna want him to think that she hates you. It'll cause problems for their marriage. Ava went through all this to get your dad. I don't think she wants to mess up."

"I don't need Ava pretending to like me for Jerome's sake. I'd rather be left out of the equation."

"What if she's not pretending?" Alyssa asks. "What if she really wants to get to know you, Divine?"

I shrug in nonchalance. "I don't know. We'll just have to wait and see. Take one day at a time."

AUNT PHOEBE LOOKS like a polka-dot magnet on the following Sunday.

She's wearing a black-and-white polka-dot dress, matching hat, shoes, and purse—how in the world did she manage to find that in one place? I wonder. Aunt Phoebe went shopping yesterday to get some new clothes. I knew I should've gone with her. She's dangerous when left shopping on her own.

I chew on my bottom lip to keep from bursting into laughter

when Uncle Reed does a double take when he walks into the kitchen. I wait to see if he's going to say anything about her outfit.

To my disappointment, he doesn't.

Alyssa can't resist, however. She walks into the kitchen and says, "Where did they find all those polka dots to put on your outfit?"

I howl with laughter.

Aunt Phoebe eyes Alyssa a moment before responding, "I'm sorry they didn't have any left over for you—your skirt could use a few." She glances over at me. "What about you, Miss Fashion Diva? C'mon, get it out."

"I wasn't going to say anything, but since you asked—I'll tell you. I think if you just put on a black hat, change into some black shoes, and carry a black purse, you'll look fierce. If you want to do the polka-dot accessories, then just wear a black dress. This way, you break up all the polka dots. Right now . . . Aunt Phoebe, you got a lot going on. It's like, way too much. I see spots everywhere after I look at your outfit."

Aunt Phoebe touches her hat. "I really like my hat and I wanted to wear it today. It matches my dress perfectly."

"Do you have a black blazer you can wear over the dress?" I ask.

Aunt Phoebe nods.

"Then put that on. It'll break up the dots some. I still say a solid black dress is the way to go."

Alyssa nods in agreement as if she really knows anything about fashion. She's not much better than Aunt Phoebe.

Aunt Phoebe walks out of the kitchen, leaving us to wonder if we hurt her feelings. Uncle Reed takes off after her.

"Do you think we made her mad?" I ask. "I didn't mean to hurt her feelings."

"I hope not," answers Alyssa.

When Aunt Phoebe returns, she looks like a different person. She's now wearing a long-sleeve black dress with a double strand of pearls. She's determined to wear the polka-dot hat and shoes. I gaze at her face, trying to see if she's upset with me.

She breaks into a smile. "I think I like this look better, sugar."

I release a short sigh of relief. *Thank you, Jesus.*

I sure don't want to be on her bad side. I don't need Aunt Phoebe coming out the box on me right before church. I like to go to church in a good mood. I'm not sure why—I just feel that's the way it needs to be.

We leave for church fifteen minutes later. Uncle Reed and Chance ride together while Alyssa and I ride over with Aunt Phoebe.

"Madison's coming to church this morning," I announce.

"We'll be glad to see him."

"Aunt Phoebe, what do you think of Madison really? I mean, do you like him as much as you like Stephen?"

She nods. "He's a nice young man. I like that he seems to really care about you. Your uncle and I are pleased with your choice in friends. You and Alyssa have done well."

"So are you willing to reconsider letting them come visit us at the house?"

"Divine . . . Madison and Stephen are not going anywhere. You don't have to be in such a rush."

"I'm getting older. I could die tomorrow, you know. How would you like to die without ever having been on a real date?"

"The way I see it, you can't miss what you never had."

"Aunt Phoebe, you're not being fair. I got you looking all fierce for church. You know all the other women will be hatin' on you big-time today. Fashion expertise doesn't exactly come cheap."

She laughs.

"Divine, just give it up," Alyssa tells me. "You know Mama's not gonna change her mind."

"Just thought I'd give it one more shot."

"Sugar, look what happened to Mia. Maybe if she were a little older when she started keeping company with boys, she might have handled her situation a little better."

I hadn't considered that. "I guess."

Aunt Phoebe pulls into the church parking lot and parks right beside Uncle Reed's car.

Alyssa and I climb out of the van and follow Aunt Phoebe into the sanctuary. Madison and Stephen are already there and seated toward the back, near the exit doors.

Aunt Phoebe gestures for them to come up front. "Y'all know you not gon' be sitting way in the back like that. Come on up here with us."

I can't believe she's doing this. Talk about embarrassing.

Madison gives Aunt Phoebe a hug. He doesn't get upset when she does stuff like that. He just laughs and does whatever she says. Stephen, on the other hand, rolls his eyes heavenward. He greets my aunt with a handshake. I can tell Alyssa's a little bothered by it. She's going to pull him to the side as soon as she gets a chance and tell him off. I just know it. She wants him to stay on Aunt Phoebe's good side.

I lean over and whisper, "Don't be too hard on him."

"He could've hugged her, too. I bet you that Mama's gonna say something about it. She don't miss nothing."

We take our seats beside Stephen and Madison seconds before church service starts. Aunt Phoebe sits in the aisle across from us.

She may not be looking directly at us, but I'm pretty sure she's got a camera zoomed in on our seats. Aunt Phoebe's not going to miss a beat when it comes to Alyssa and me.

Uncle Reed's eyes are glued on us through most of the service, however. This morning the topic of his sermon is singleness in Christ. Alyssa and I glance at each other. Talk about a major coincidence. Aunt Phoebe always says there are no coincidences. She says everything is designed by God. I guess Madison and Stephen are supposed to be here to hear what Uncle Reed has to say about the subject.

"The biggest question most young people have today is, why does God give us such powerful hormones now, if we aren't supposed to get married for years? The reason I decided to talk about this is to show that God didn't make a mistake when he made us. Song of Solomon chapter three, verse five, says, do not stir up, do not arouse love before its own time. Unfortunately, the media stirs up those desires in not just our teens, but in all of us. Research shows that we see over fourteen thousand sexual references and innuendos on television each year."

Aunt Phoebe glances over at us.

"I want you to know that God has given you these sexual desires. But we also have to learn to control them."

It's not that easy, I think to myself. I know how Madison makes me feel just being around him. My heart races and I get this little tingle in my tummy.

". . . We begin to get emotionally closer, and our bodies desire the same closeness," Uncle Reed is saying.

I steal a peek at Madison. He seems genuinely interested in what my uncle is saying.

I turn my attention back to Uncle Reed.

"There is absolutely nothing wrong with becoming friends and spending time with members of the opposite sex. But when we do enter into relationships, we should allow wisdom to chaperone romance. This involves having the humility to become accountable to others. Find a member of the same sex that you look up to and go to him or her for guidance in your relationships. Proverbs chapter fifteen, verse twenty-two, says, without counsel plans go wrong, but with many advisers they succeed. It's a good idea to spend time together with the other person's family. Young people, I want you to remember this: how a person treats his or her family will most likely be how he or she treats you when the feelings taper off. For example, if you are a young woman dating a guy who is disrespectful toward his mother and sisters, guess what you have to look forward to?"

Thoughts of Mia enter my mind. I'd heard that Tim curses out his grandmother and that she had to call the police on him a couple of times.

"If we spend every waking hour snuggled up together and gazing into our sweetheart's eyes, we will never find out who they are. The *type* of time that a boy and girl spend together is essential if you wish to know what kind of person you're dealing with. Spending time in service, with family, and even playing sports will help reveal who the person really is. Young people, I hope you know what I'm saying. Before entering in a relationship, ask for God's blessing. Enter into that relationship with direction toward a certain purpose. Involve the families; be accountable to others; and pace yourselves as you spend time together. Don't let your emotions take control. Most of all, you both should always listen for the Lord's guidance."

When the service ends, Madison tells me, "I like what your uncle had to say. It helps me with some things I was dealing with. Mostly, I got it. It made sense to me."

"I'm glad. I feel the same way."

Aunt Phoebe comes over to where we're all standing. "I hope you boys will consider joining us for Sunday dinner."

Alyssa and I both nearly faint from the shock. Aunt Phoebe is actually inviting Madison and Stephen to eat with us? Then I recall

Uncle Reed's words: it's a good idea to spend time together with the other person's family.

I smile. "Madison, will you call your parents and see if you can come?"

"I don't think it'll be a problem," he responds. "Thanks for the invitation, Mrs. Matthews."

This time Stephen gives Aunt Phoebe a hug. "Thank you so much," he says.

She laughs. "I'll expect you both around two. Don't be late."

I turn to Madison when Aunt Phoebe leaves. "Wow. I can't believe she's letting you and Stephen come over for dinner. I don't know what brought this on, but I'm loving it."

"I want to be with you, Divine. And if I have to join this church to prove it to your family, I will."

When he flashes that sexy grin of his, my heart melts.

Aunt Phoebe comes back over to get me and Alyssa, saying, "Girls, we need to get home. We're having guests for dinner, so we need to leave."

"I'll see you at two," I tell Madison.

"I'll be there. *On time.*"

Once we get to the van, I say, "Aunt Phoebe, I love you. Thanks so much for doing this."

"Yeah," Alyssa contributes. "We owe you big-time."

"Just don't make me ever regret it."

"We won't," we vow in unison.

Aunt Phoebe has a heart after all.

I WAKE UP Monday morning with a big grin on my face. Aunt Phoebe cooked a fabulous meal yesterday and I was able to spend most of the afternoon with Madison. We played Scrabble after dinner and Madison won.

Uncle Reed had a point about doing things together. I hadn't realized just how smart Madison really is until I saw what a whiz he is with words. I learned something new about him.

I get dressed for school and head to the kitchen to have breakfast.

Alyssa and Chance are sitting at the table with Uncle Reed. Aunt Phoebe's at the stove making pancakes and sausage.

"What did everybody do?" I ask. "Get up an hour earlier?" I'm usually in the kitchen before Chance and Alyssa.

"Mama's making blueberry pancakes," Alyssa explains. "We didn't want to have to rush and eat. I want to savor my food. You know she don't make blueberry pancakes too often."

I pick up a plate and weigh it down with three pancakes and two sausage links and carry it over to the table. I sit down across from Chance, who looks like he's in a bad mood.

"You okay?" I ask him.

He eyes me. "Yeah."

We finish off our breakfast and get ready to leave for school.

On the way, I ask Chance a second time, "What's up with you? You sure you're okay?"

"I'm fine. Just sick of Trina's parents trying to cut me out of my son's life."

"What are they doing now?" Alyssa inquires.

"They're trying to tell me when I can see Joshua. I wanted to go by and see him after school since I don't have to work tonight, but they're going to see Trina's aunt or somebody. This is the only day I'm not working. I offered to take him to my house until they get back. Mrs. Winston's still trying to say Joshua's too young. He needs to be with Trina because she's breast-feeding."

"Well, I can understand that."

"She pumps her milk into bottles," Chance states. "I can feed my son. Mama and Daddy are going to talk to the Winstons. I deserve to spend time with Joshua."

"Well, what is Trina saying about all this?" I want to know.

"All she keeps saying is that we wouldn't have this problem if we get our own place after we graduate or if we get married."

"I know she not trying to punk you," I say without thinking. "Oooh, nooo. Not my cousin."

Alyssa shakes her head. "Trina's wrong for that."

"She's changed since she had Joshua. She act like she's calling all the shots now."

"You think? Chance, she's trying to manipulate you." I switch my backpack from one shoulder to the other. "Trina don't know who she messing with. You better show her, Chance. Don't you let her talk you into doing something you don't want to do. I like Trina, but she's been pulling your chain since she got pregnant."

Alyssa agrees. "I'm beginning to think she got pregnant on purpose."

"I think so, too," Chance practically whispers. "I'ma have a talk with her later on tonight. I love my son and I love Trina, but if she don't make some changes . . . we won't be together. I'ma still help out and spend time with Joshua."

"Chance, we got your back," I say.

If Trina doesn't get her act together, she's about to lose the best guy a girl could have. Chance has stuck by her from the moment she told him that she was pregnant. A lot of girls aren't so lucky. I truly hope she didn't trap him deliberately. Chance will never forgive her if he finds out she did.

Chance abandons us the moment we set foot on campus.

"I don't know what to think about Trina," Alyssa whispers. "Do you think she got pregnant on purpose to trap my brother?"

"It's possible," I say. "She was having issues with him going off to Georgetown University. She could've done it to keep him down here."

"I have a feeling they might not survive this. I'm not sure my friendship with her will survive either. I don't want nobody playing my brother."

I agree. Trina's going to have to deal with us if we discover that she was trying to punk Chance.

chapter 17

I spend the weekend with Mom because she'll be leaving soon to film a new movie in Canada. She's going to be away for the next six or eight weeks.

We get up on Saturday morning and, after breakfast, head straight to the mall.

"How about this one?" Mom asks, holding up a blue-and-gold sweater. "This is nice."

"It's okay. I like this one better." I hold up a black sweater with lace trim.

"*That is nice*. Do they have one my size?"

"Mom, let's not do the 'dress alike' thing. It's so done."

She laughs. "Okay. But if you decide not to get it—let me know. I really *really* like it."

"Then you get it. I'll be able to find something else."

"You sure?"

"Yes, ma'am. The sweater's cute but it's not like I'll die if I don't have it."

Mom adds it to the other clothes she found for herself. "How is that darling little Joshua doing?"

"He's so sweet, Mom. I thought he was going to drive me crazy with all his crying, but he hardly cries. He's a good baby."

"That's what Phoebe was telling me. She says that Chance and Trina have adjusted well with Joshua."

"Chance is having a problem with Trina and her parents."

Mom meets my gaze. "What kind of problem?"

"They won't let him bring the baby home for a overnight stay. Joshua can't come to the house without Trina."

"Really?"

"They keep telling Chance that Joshua's too young and that he needs to be with Trina."

"She's breast-feeding, right?"

"Yes, ma'am, but she pumps the milk into a bottle."

Mom holds up a pair of pants against her. She looks over at me. "What do you think?"

I nod in approval.

"So what does Trina have to say?"

"She told Chance that it wouldn't be like that if they were married or had an apartment together."

"She's trying to manipulate the situation."

"Chance feels the same way. They had a long talk the other night. I don't know how it went, but I don't think it went too well. I heard him tell Alyssa yesterday that Trina hadn't returned his phone calls."

"I hope they work it out," Mom states. "They have a little boy together and they're gonna have to find a way to get along, so that they can raise that beautiful baby together."

"Mom, I hope you don't have any ideas on being a grandmother. I don't think it's going to happen—actually, I'm pretty sure I won't be having children. Seeing Trina in all that pain did it for me."

Mom laughs. "That's what you say now."

"I mean it. I don't like any kind of pain. I'm way too cute to be spread all out like that."

"And humble."

A couple of people recognize Mom and venture over asking for autographs. Mom is cool because she signs their scraps of paper and is polite, flashing that million-dollar smile everyone talks about.

"I think maybe we should check out one of the other stores. Let's get out of here."

"Ahhh . . . the disadvantages of being famous," I tease.

After a day of some serious shopping, we relax by having dinner at one of my favorite restaurants, the Cheesecake Factory, where I order the Cajun Chicken Littles and Mom orders the jambalaya.

"How is Madison?" Mom inquires when my cell phone rings.

I check the caller ID and laugh. "He's fine. How did you know it was him calling?"

"Do I really have to answer that?"

I laugh. "He loves me."

"I remember the very first time I thought I was in love. His name was Lenny Brown and talk about good-looking . . . that was a good-looking boy."

"How old were you?"

"About your age. Lenny lived two blocks from our house and he used to walk me home. But when we were about a block away— he would cross the street. He was afraid of my mama. I don't blame him. I was pretty scared of her myself."

I regret that I never had a chance to meet my grandmother. From everything I've heard about her, Addie Matthews was a force to be reckoned with, but she possessed a fierce love for her children.

"How long did you go together?"

"Almost the entire school year." Mom broke into a short laugh. "Back then, that was like a lifetime."

"Why'd you two break up?" I bite into my corn on the cob.

"He lost interest in me." Mom takes a sip of water. "There were girls who could go out and they would give him what I wouldn't."

"He broke your heart?"

Mom takes a sip of water. "I was hurt, but in the end—he was the one losing out. Lenny continued chasing skirts until it landed him in the grave."

Wiping my mouth with the edge of my napkin, I ask, "What do you mean? Did somebody kill him?"

"Something killed him. Lenny died of AIDS-related complications."

"That sucks big-time." I stab a chicken nugget with my fork and stick it in the honey-mustard sauce before eating it.

Mom agrees. "For that brief time we were together—if you can call it that—he made me smile. Lenny made me happy."

I settle back in my chair. "So you're saying that I should enjoy the time I have with Madison because things could change."

"Some people are only in our lives for a season, hon. You make the most of the time you have together. Make lots of happy memories."

"Uncle Reed and Aunt Phoebe were childhood sweethearts. It's possible Madison and I could stay together a long time."

"I agree." Mom wipes her mouth before continuing. "Divine, honey . . . I just want you to enjoy your life. Stop trying to grow up so quickly. Being a grown-up is not all it's cracked up to be—it's actually harder than being a kid."

"You get to do whatever you want."

"And you think that's fun? What about all the responsibility that comes with that?"

"Well, it's fun some of the time, right?"

Mom smiles at me. "Yeah. It can be fun sometimes."

She passes on dessert but I'm not about to miss out on the huge slice of Black Forest cake. It'll take me two days to eat it, but it's so worth it.

Mom pays the check and we leave.

"Where's Kevin this weekend?" I inquire when we're in the car and on the way home. "Is he out of town?"

"No, he's here in Atlanta. He wanted to give us some mother-daughter time alone. Kevin knows I'll be leaving town on Tuesday."

"He must be trying to score points with you."

Mom pinches me. "Stop that."

I laugh. But then I notice that Mom seems to have a certain kind of look. Especially when she talks about Kevin.

When we're at home, I follow Mom into her room. "Mom, can we talk?"

"Sure, hon. We can sit here in the sitting room."

I sit down on the burgundy sofa, gathering the ivory-colored cashmere throw around me. "I think we need to have a serious talk about Kevin. I know we've discussed him before, but I sense that something has changed. I think you're falling in love with him."

"You've always been very perceptive. The truth is that I think you're right. Somewhere along my getting to know Kevin and building a friendship, I fell for him."

I groan. "Mom, you were supposed to tell me that I was wrong. You should've just denied it."

She wraps an arm around me. "You don't have anything to worry about, hon. You are my daughter and I love you dearly, but my heart is big enough to love you and Kevin."

I give her a sidelong glance. "So does this mean that he's going to be here all the time now?"

"You mean like move in?"

I nod.

Mom shakes her head no. "Kevin's not moving in, Divine. He won't be spending the night either. In fact, we've both agreed to practice celibacy."

"That's a relief."

"Divine, I'd like for you to do me a favor."

"What is it?"

"Please give Kevin a chance. Just get to know him. I care a great deal for him, and I really want your support. You and I are a team. You can't control my life, but I really want you to be happy."

"I will. If it really means that much to you. I just hope you don't rush off and get married like Jerome did. I need time to adjust . . . you know? I've had way too many changes in my life in a short time. I'm still a kid."

"Oh, now you want to be a kid," Mom says with a grin.

Uncle Reed wants to talk to me after Mom drops me off on Sunday evening. I meet him in his office.

"Whatever it is—I didn't do it," I exclaim, taking a seat on the black leather sofa. "It must have been Chance or Alyssa."

"Feeling guilty about something?" he asks with a grin.

I laugh. My uncle doesn't really say a whole lot except when he's in the pulpit or lecturing one of us, but he's a real good listener. Aunt Phoebe is a good listener, too, but sometimes I just like talking to Uncle Reed.

"I've been thinking about something," I begin. "Uncle Reed, I really think you should offer self-defense classes at the church. Every since Mia's drama, I haven't been able to get it off my mind."

Uncle Reed agrees. "I'll talk to the board, but I'm sure it won't be a problem."

"If you offer them, how much are they going to cost?"

"They will be free."

"Really?"

He nods.

"Can Mia take the classes even though she's not a member of our church?" I know how bad she wants to be able to defend herself.

"Of course she can."

"She's going to be so excited. Thanks so much, Uncle Reed." Another question comes to mind. "Is this just for teens?"

"I'm thinking women of all ages would be able to benefit from the classes."

I agree. "This is so good. I can't wait to tell Mia. I'm going to call her tonight."

"Once we have all the information and a schedule prepared, I'll have flyers made."

"I can distribute them at the school. Does Alyssa know about this?"

"Not yet. I thought I'd tell you first since you were the one lobbying for the classes."

"Thank you for listening to me, Uncle Reed. Sometimes you can be so cool." I rise to my feet. "Can I go tell Alyssa?"

"Sure."

I leave Uncle Reed's office humming to myself.

"Guess what, Alyssa," I say, walking into her room without knocking.

"This better be good," she tells me. "I'm on the phone with Stephen."

"It is. Uncle Reed's going to hold self-defense classes at the church."

"Stephen, I'll give you a call back." Alyssa clicks off. "When did this happen?"

"I guess today. He just told me."

"I'm gonna be the first to sign up. What about you? Are you planning on taking the classes, Divine?"

"We can take them together. It'll be fun."

After my conversation with Alyssa, I go down to my room and call Mia to share the good news with her.

"I can't wait," she squeals. "When do the classes start?"

"I don't know. Uncle Reed says that they have to do a schedule and find the people to conduct the classes."

"I can't believe I actually thought you were just trying to break up me and Tim."

"Why would I want to do that?"

"I don't know. I just thought you were jealous of us. But now I see that it was only because you really care about me."

"You really thought I was jealous of you and Tim?"

"Yeah. Probably because that's what he kept telling me. Divine, he even said that you liked him and was mad that he chose me."

"He was dreaming. I hope you didn't fall for that lie."

"Not really. I knew you were really into Madison."

I hear a click and check my phone. I'm surprised to see Trina's name pop up. She and I don't normally talk much, and when we do, it's usually on the landline phone. I tell Mia, "I need to take this. Can I call you back?"

"I'll be here at home. Holla."

"Trina . . ."

"Hey, Divine. Are you busy?"

"Not at the moment. What's up?"

"Has Chance talked to you about me?"

"Excuse me?"

"Does Chance talk to you about me? The reason I'm asking is

because he seems to think that I got pregnant on purpose and I'm trying to manipulate him using my son."

"And you're calling me why?"

I can hear Trina's sigh of frustration.

"Divine, he's been talking to someone."

"You don't think Chance can think for himself? Trina, he's not stupid." I climb out of my bed and walk down to Alyssa's room. I put a finger to my lips to silence her.

"What's going on?" she mouths.

"I'm not saying that, Divine. It's just strange to me that Chance all of a sudden is accusing me of trapping him."

"Trina, I'm still not sure why you're calling me."

"Because this sounds like something you'd tell him."

"Well, for your information, I didn't say anything to Chance. If I did, I'd have no problem telling you I said it."

"I'm not accusing you, Divine. I'm just asking. I'm trying to figure out why Chance is tripping."

"It sounds to me as if you two have a lot to discuss."

"I feel like I'm losing him and I don't know what to do about it."

"Maybe you shouldn't try to do anything, Trina. Just give Chance some space. He loves Joshua and he wants to be a good father. Let him do what he can."

She starts to cry. "I don't want to lose him."

"He loves you. Trina, you guys are still young. Don't try to rush into something that you'll regret."

"Divine, you don't get it. Chance is the father of my child. We have a son together. We are a family. I just want to make sure I don't lose my family. He wants to go off to college, but he has a responsibility to me and Joshua."

"Trina, what are you saying?"

"Chance and I are a family. We should get married. I'm not

talking about right this minute. We can do it after we graduate, but it's the right thing to do. If he loves Joshua as much as he says—why doesn't he want to be with us?"

"Maybe because he's not ready for that type of commitment. Trina, you really should be discussing this with Chance."

"He doesn't want to talk about marriage. All Chance is thinking about is going off to school."

"He's going to Morehouse or Clark. That's in Atlanta. He's not going to be that far away."

"I told him that Joshua and I could move to Atlanta with him. He doesn't want us there."

"It sounds like he doesn't want to live in sin, Trina."

Alyssa rolls her eyes heavenward. I know she's seriously tripping off what she's hearing. She's my witness if any drama comes up. I'm not sure I trust Trina anymore.

She keeps me on the phone for another half hour. I'm all talked out because we keep going around in circles. I'm convinced after this conversation that Trina got pregnant on purpose because she thought it would make Chance marry her.

When we get off the phone, Alyssa says, "She sounds like she's losing it."

I agree. "Maybe it's her hormones."

"I feel like calling Trina and telling her off."

The telephone rings.

"It's Trina," Alyssa says. "She knows Chance is at work."

"Answer it."

She shakes her head no. "I don't have nothing to say to her."

I hear Chance talking as he walks down the hall and say, "I didn't know he was here."

"I didn't either. I thought he was still at work."

Instead of going into his room and closing the door like he

usually does, Chance joins us in Alyssa's room. He takes a seat on the edge of her bed.

"Why did you call Divine? She don't have nothing to do with us."

I can tell by the tone of his voice that Chance isn't pleased with this piece of news. It's about to be on and poppin'. Best part is that Alyssa and I have a front-row seat.

"Trina, I've told you before that I love you. I really do. But I'm not ready to get married . . . Yeah, I know we have a child together. If we are still together when I graduate college—we'll get married. I'm not changing my mind."

Alyssa and I exchange looks.

"Trina, there is no reason why I shouldn't be able to bring my son to my house. You had him out at the mall. You don't have a problem taking him there. Why can't he come here for a couple of hours? You always complaining that you don't get much sleep. Let me keep him sometime."

"All right, Chance," I murmur. I'm thrilled to see him take charge over the situation. Trina's trying to punk him but he's not having it. My cousin's not a fool.

"I want him tomorrow night if you're serious. I don't have to work. That way you can get some rest."

Chance's tone softens and he rises to his feet. When he strolls out of the room, I tell Alyssa, "She's getting to him again."

"He said what he needed to say though. Chance set Miss Trina straight."

"Yeah, he did."

I stretch and yawn. "Girl, all this drama is making me tired. I must be getting too old for this mess. I'm going to take a shower and get my clothes ready for school tomorrow."

Alyssa reaches into the top drawer of her nightstand, pulling out a blue-and-silver necklace. "You wanted to see this so that you could make a matching bracelet. I still have to make the earrings."

"Oh, yeah. I'm going to make two different bracelets. Most of our customers are buying an average of two bracelets per person. We're going to make lots of money off the sets. Just watch and see."

Stifling a yawn, I cover my mouth. "I'll give this back to you when I'm done."

After my shower, I don't feel as sleepy. I guess the hot, soapy water woke me up. I sit at my desk and surf the internet looking for charms. I have an idea for a series of charm bracelets, so I'm looking for some unusual ones.

While looking at hundreds of charms on one website, I discover an awareness-ribbon charm in several colors. When I see the dark blue one for domestic violence or child abuse, I get an idea.

TRINA ACTUALLY COMES through for Chance and allows him to bring Joshua over for a visit.

"I still can't believe you're a daddy," I say when I walk into the family room where Chance is giving Joshua a bottle. "Look at you . . ."

"I still can't believe it myself," Chance says. "I never thought in a million years that I'd be doing this before I graduated high school. My son is going to be at my graduation."

"You won't be the only one with a child in the audience."

"Still doesn't make it right."

I sit down beside him. "Does it bother you? Being a daddy?"

"I love Joshua. But I wanted to go to college and just enjoy my life without any responsibilities. That's all changed now."

I play with one of Joshua's little feet. "You'll still be able to go to college."

"Not at Georgetown University."

"You can if you want to."

Chance shakes his head no. "I'm not gonna leave Trina and Joshua. I've been accepted into Clark University, so that's where I'm going. Unless I can get into Morehouse."

"They're both good schools. Alyssa and I will be over at Spelman in a couple of years. Maybe all of us can get a nice apartment together."

"Like I want to live with the two of you."

I laugh. "You know you do."

Chance removes the bottle from his sleeping son's mouth. "Morehouse and Clark are both real good schools, but they're just not my first choice."

"Trina and Joshua will be fine if you went away to school, Chance. It's not like you won't be able to come home during the holidays and in the summer."

"I'm not going to leave Trina with the responsibility of raising Joshua and going to school. I have to be here so I can help her."

"Sounds like you've made up your mind. Just make sure that this is your decision and not Trina's."

"I have. I still have some doubts about Trina. I'm not gonna lie, but it really doesn't matter. She and I made a baby and he has to come first. I'm not leaving my son."

"Chance, don't go getting a big head or nothing after I say this, but you're pretty cool. Trina's very lucky to have you. But if you ever tell anyone I said this, I'll deny it."

Chance grins. "Hey, can you watch Joshua while I go to the bathroom?"

I nod. "I'm not changing any diapers though, so hurry up."

I sit watching Joshua as he sleeps. He's such a cute little baby. He is beginning to look more and more like Chance.

When he comes back into the family room, I leave Chance with his son.

Just as I head to my room, I hear Aunt Phoebe and Alyssa come through the garage. I pause long enough to tell them that Joshua's sleeping in the family room. My aunt can't wait to get her hands on her grandson. She instructs us to bring the groceries into the house.

I walk out with Alyssa.

"I can't believe Trina actually let Chance bring the baby over here. He must have gotten through to her last night." Alyssa picks up a plastic bag and hands it to me.

"Or she's trying to keep the peace until she can find another way to play him," I say. "Sorry, but it's going to take me a minute to trust Trina again."

chapter 18

Alyssa and I have made over $200 off our jewelry already. My bracelets are so fierce that all the girls in school want to own some. The sets that Alyssa and I put together are selling like hotcakes. Alyssa's expression—not mine.

"It's official," I tell Penny. "Alyssa and I are *jewelry designers*. Pretty soon, our stuff is going to be in all the major magazines. Now don't you feel honored just knowing us?"

"Divine, you're a nut! I don't care how famous you get or think you are—y'all nothing but family to me."

Penny's just hatin' on me and Alyssa because she doesn't have our skills. "Don't hate. Girl, we can't help our entrepreneurial spirit."

"Whatever . . ."

I laugh. "I'm going to have to make a whole bunch more. Some of the girls want me to do more bracelets for them."

"I know one thing . . . I'm going shopping," Alyssa announces.

"What are you doing with your share?" Penny asks me.

"I've been thinking about that. What do you think about me giving some of the money to the National Domestic Violence Hotline?"

"I think it's a great idea," Alyssa says. "I just read somewhere that Liz Claiborne is doing something to help prevent teen violence."

"Yeah. I read something about that. That's so cool."

"Hey, I heard that Mia's parents took out a restraining order against Tim," Penny states. "If he comes anywhere near her—he'll go to jail. I haven't seen him in a minute, so maybe he moved back to Birmingham."

"Good. I knew they were planning to do it, but didn't know if they had. I try not to mention Tim to Mia. She still has feelings for him."

"He's not supposed to even be on our campus anymore," Alyssa states. "His grandmother withdrew him from school. I heard she told the principal that she couldn't handle him, so she was definitely sending him back to his mama."

"That's a relief. I know Mia will be happy."

As luck would have it, I run straight into Tim right after my first-period class. He gives me a dirty look but doesn't say anything.

I see Alyssa in the sea of students going from one class to the other. I rush over to her, saying, "I just saw Tim. He's here on campus. Do you know where Mia is?"

Alyssa shakes her head no. "I haven't seen her. What is he doing here?"

I shrug. "I don't know. I just hope Mia doesn't see him. That's the last thing she needs right now."

We go searching for Mia and locate her coming out of the library.

"Hey, y'all," she greets.

Alyssa and I exchange looks. I totally don't know what to say at this point. I don't want to upset my friend but she needs to know.

Mia eyes me. "Divine, what's wrong?"

"Don't freak, but I just saw Tim."

"Did he say something to you?"

I see stark fear in her eyes now. Mia's still very much afraid of him. It reminds me of how I felt when Theopolis Mack was still alive. I couldn't really feel safe until I heard that he was dead.

"Divine, did he say anything?" Mia asks a second time.

"No. He just gave me this dirty look, but he didn't open his mouth, which is a first."

"Do you think he's still on the campus? My parents took out a restraining order and he's not supposed to be here at all."

"Why don't we go to the office?" I suggest. "You should probably call your dad. I just don't trust Tim."

I leave Mia in the office and get a late pass to enter my second-period class. I run into Mia at her locker when the bell rings. "Did you call your dad?"

"Uh-huh. He's on his way here." Mia takes her jacket out of her locker. "He says he's going to pull me out of this school until he's sure Tim is gone and I'm safe. He said they may enroll me in another school. I don't want to leave all my friends, but Divine, I'm so scared."

Nicholas joins us. "Hey, I just saw Tim leaving campus. You okay, Mia?"

"For now."

"I'll walk you up to the office," he offers.

During lunch, I update Alyssa. "So she's not coming back to school until her parents are sure she'll be safe. They're even thinking about enrolling her in another school permanently."

"They must be moving out of Temple."

"What are you talking about, Alyssa?"

"I heard that their house was for sale. It doesn't have a sign in the yard, but it's on the market."

"Who told you that? Mia hasn't said anything to me."

"Tina Gilyard's mom is the real estate agent. They are trying to keep it quiet. I'm not supposed to know, so don't say anything. Just wait for Mia to tell you."

Nicholas walks by our table and waves.

"I think Nicholas likes Mia," Alyssa announces. "Have you noticed how protective he is of her?"

"Not really. He's asked me about her a couple of times, but I thought he was just making conversation. Guess that's why he's never really tried to be with me like that."

"You're not upset about it, are you? Because you sound a little disappointed."

"Who, me?" I shake my head no. "Girl, please. I have Madison."

Alyssa eats her hamburger while I devour my salad.

"Trina's coming back to school next week," she announces.

I shrug in nonchalance. I'm still a little cool where she's concerned. Trina's been on her best behavior since she and Chance had that talk, but I'm curious to see how long she's going to lie low. I see her in an entirely different light now.

"You don't like her anymore. Do you?"

I meet Alyssa's gaze. "I don't really know how I feel about her. She can't be playing Chance."

"I think he's got everything under control."

"We'll see."

AFTER I PUT away the last of my laundry, I call Rhyann. The last time I talked to her, she was still steaming over her breakup with Carson. Mimi had sent me a text message to tell me that Rhyann got in trouble for breaking the windshield of his car with a rock.

She answers the phone on the second ring.

"Dee, I'm not supposed to be on the phone, but Auntie Mama is at the grocery store. If I hang up on you, it's because she's come back."

"Rhyann, what were you thinking?"

"He was cheating on me. I can't let that idiot play me like that."

"Did he really call the police on you?"

"Yeah. Can you believe it? But that's all right. My brothers are on their way to have a talk with him. He's going to drop the charges. I can promise you that."

"I don't want to see you on the news, Rhyann. That boy is so not worth your time. There are a lot of guys out there who would love to have you as a girlfriend."

"Oh, I already met my next boyfriend. His name is Trey. Girl, he is so fine."

Okay, I'm confused. "Rhyann, if you've met someone else, why are you breaking windshields? I'm not getting it."

"Because then Carson will think twice before he tries to dog out another girl."

"Rhyann . . ."

"What? I gave that boy my heart, Dee. He didn't treat me right so I broke his windshield. I think it's more than fair. I could've had my brothers beat him up or worse."

"Well, I'm glad you didn't. The windshield is enough. Now you can move on with Trey."

"Dee, I've gotta go. Auntie Mama just pulled in the driveway. I'll try and email you later."

We end the call.

I walk down the hall to Alyssa's room. "Girl, you won't believe what Rhyann did."

Alyssa looks up from the magazine she was reading. "What?"

"She smashed her ex-boyfriend's windshield with a rock. He called the police on her and pressed charges."

"For real?"

I nod. "But get this. Rhyann's met somebody else. She must have really liked Carson because the girl clearly has lost her mind. I can't believe she did that."

"Well, you were pretty mad when Madison dumped you. You wanted to hurt him good."

"But I didn't. Besides, that was last year. I'm much more mature now."

Alyssa cracks up laughing.

I throw a pillow at her, hitting her right in the chest. She picks up one, planning to return the favor.

I duck.

Laughing, I run out of Alyssa's room.

"My parents are selling our house," Mia announces when she comes over. Aunt Phoebe's taking a group of us to the mall so that we can start the search for our prom dresses.

Mia and I sit in the family room waiting on Alyssa to finish getting ready and for Trina and Penny to arrive.

"We heard that Tim is back in Birmingham, but my dad isn't so sure he won't come back here. They're worried that he might try to burn the house down or kill us in our sleep."

I almost choke on my soda. "Do you think he's that dangerous?"

I instantly regret my question. Like, duh . . . he broke her arm. I sure hope Mia's arm will be out of that ugly cast by the time prom comes around. It'll stick out like a sore thumb in her pictures.

Mia shrugs. "I don't know, but my parents don't want to take any chances with my life."

"Are you leaving Temple?"

She nods. "My dad just got a real nice job in Atlanta. We were there over the weekend and found a house there. It's got five bedrooms and a three-car garage. I'm kinda sad about leaving y'all, but you know how much I love Atlanta."

"I'm going to miss you."

"Divine, I'm definitely gonna miss you, too. You've been a real good friend to me. Guess what? I might be able to take tae kwon do classes now."

"That's great, Mia."

Alyssa walks into the family room. "Trina and Penny should be here soon. Stacy's going to meet us there. She's still at the hairdresser."

Alyssa and Mia hug, then sit down side by side.

"Mia just told me that she's moving to Atlanta."

"Oh, we're gonna miss you. But we'll get to see you when we go to Aunt Kara's house."

"Please don't tell anyone. My parents want to keep it on the down low. They are worried that Tim could still be here or that he'll come back looking for me."

Alyssa nods in understanding. "I won't tell anyone."

"Do you know when you're moving?"

"I'm gonna finish school here. We'll be moving right after school lets out."

"So what do you think of Nicholas?" I ask Mia.

"He's nice. We've been talking a lot more lately. In fact, he's asked me to go to the prom with him."

This is news to me. Nicholas and I were in class this morning and he never said a word. "So what are you going to do? Are you going with him?"

"I am. I plan on having a good time at the prom. I love dancing and Nicholas can dance—did you see him at the Valentine's dance?"

I nod in agreement. "He's one of the best dancers at the school. You should see him in our tae kwon do classes. He's real good."

"I was thinking all this time that Nicholas was interested in you."

"You mean he wasn't?" I tease.

"I'm serious. I think he had a crush on you in the beginning, but Nicholas knew he didn't stand a chance with you."

"He and I are just good friends."

"Well, I'm not rushing into anything with Nicholas. I like talking to him though."

"Nothing wrong with that," I say. "Have you told him that you're moving?"

She nods. "He says it doesn't matter to him. He goes to Atlanta all the time to visit with his brother. His brother attends Clark University. As a matter of fact, that's where Nicholas and I are applying. We both want to go to Clark. Isn't that amazing?"

She's sitting here with this big grin on her face. Alyssa and I look at each other and burst into laughter.

"What?" she asks.

"I wish you could see your face," I say. "You have this big grin on your face. I think you got puppy-dog love for Nicholas."

"You're one to talk. You're the one with the puppy-dog look whenever Madison's around."

I shake my head no. "No puppy love here. Girl, I got big-dog love for my boo."

"It feels good not being so tense all of the time. Nicholas doesn't trip if I have to call him back or anything. He's not demanding at all. I'm tripping because I've never met a boy like him before."

"Just enjoy the time you have with him, Mia. Make lots of happy memories."

"I want a boyfriend, but I'm not gonna rush it," Mia vows. "That's where I always go wrong. I get impatient."

Trina arrives with Joshua.

"I'm sorry I'm late. Joshua had to boo-boo just as we were about to leave. He got some on my clothes, so I had to change him and then change me."

Alyssa takes the sleeping baby out of Trina's arms and carries him to Chance.

Trina walks over to me and sits down. "I feel like there's something going on between us," she says. "Did I do something to upset you?"

I meet her gaze straight on. "Trina, I know how much my cousin cares for you. He's crazy about you. I just don't want you to hurt him. If you do, then we're going to have a problem. I hope we understand each other."

She nods. "Divine, I love Chance. I love him with my whole heart."

"Then you need to trust that love."

Chance walks into the room, putting an end to our conversation. Trina rises to her feet and walks over to him.

"Where's the diaper bag?" he asks.

"I left it by the front door," Trina responds. They walk up to the front of the house.

Penny is the last one to arrive. That girl is never on time for anything.

We pile into the van ten minutes later.

"Aunt Phoebe, you been looking pretty cute lately," Penny says. "What did you do? Go out and get a new wardrobe?"

"My little fashion advisers back there helped me clean out my closet a few weeks back."

We arrive twenty minutes later at the Arbor Place Mall in Douglasville.

"I'll be back here at six o'clock. If you get finished before then, just call me and I'll come back and pick y'all up."

"Thanks, Mama," Alyssa tells her.

I wave as she pulls off.

"I can't wait to get a car," Trina says. "It's so embarrassing to have to wait on your parents to take you everywhere."

I totally agree. "I thought I'd have a car by now, but Mom says I won't get one until I get ready to go off to college. That's like so totally unfair."

"Yeah, totally," Penny mimicks.

"You're so mature," I utter.

We walk around the mall, stopping from time to time to check out prom dresses. Penny finds a pale blue one she just can't live without. Personally, I think it's ugly and the color is all wrong for her, but she refuses to listen to me. She'll never be prom queen in that dress.

"I don't like any of these dresses," Alyssa says. "I'ma have to wait until we go to Atlanta to find one."

Trina releases a long sigh. "I saw a black one in the last store that I liked, but I wanted to make sure it's the one I want before I buy it. Maybe I should go back and try it on."

"Are you talking about the one that looked like a nightgown?" I ask.

"It looked like a nightgown to you?"

I nod. "My mom has one that's very similar to it. Trina, I'm sure you can find something better."

We stop and wait for Mia to get her Auntie Anne's pretzel. She loves them with lots of mustard. I give in to my curiosity and order one of the original pretzels. I have to see if I've been missing something.

I sample my pretzel. "Mmmm, this is good. I like it with the mustard."

"I told you they were good."

Inspired, Alyssa orders the original pretzel sticks and Trina gets the cinnamon sugar.

Penny decides to pass on the snack. "I'm waiting for some real food."

We venture into Parisian.

"I'm not sure we're going to find anything we can afford in here," Trina states. "Well, maybe Divine will find something."

"Keep an open mind," I reply. "They have some good sales from time to time."

"I have a two-hundred-dollar budget," Mia states.

Alyssa laughs. "We all have a two-hundred-dollar budget. Mine includes my shoes, purse . . . whatever."

"I have my dress," Penny says. "I just need to find the perfect shoes."

We take the escalator to the Social Occasion department, running our mouths the entire time.

"See," I say, pointing to a rack a few yards away, "they have some dresses on sale."

We comb through the clothes, looking for that special something. I strike out. Today is just not a good day for me. Maybe I should call Mom and see if I can have something original—especially designed for me. Most likely Mom will refuse. She says I have to be more sensitive about Alyssa's feelings when it comes to stuff like this.

Why? Alyssa knows that I'm rich.

Mia finds a red dress made up of ruffles and a red satin bow. She goes off to one of the dressing rooms and tries it on.

"It looks cute on you," I tell her. "Mia, I really like it."

Alyssa and Trina murmur their approval.

Penny scans Mia from head to toe. "I don't like ruffles personally, but it's nice on you. I think you should get it."

Alyssa's cell phone rings.

It's Stacy, so Alyssa tells her where we are.

When she gets off the phone, she announces, "Stacy's coming up. She was standing right outside this store."

Stacy arrives minutes later, her shoulder-length hair looking fly in a wrapped style. I wish she wouldn't go home and put all those rollers in it. I actually like her hair better when she wears it like this.

I'm so thankful to have been born with a sense of style. So many people are clueless when it comes to fashion dos and don'ts.

Trina holds a black dress against her body. "What do you think about this one?"

"You're set on wearing black, aren't you?" I question.

"What's wrong with black? I haven't lost all of my baby weight. It'll make me look smaller."

"Trina, I hate to tell you this, but you're the same size in black as you are in any other color."

"I really didn't need you to tell me that."

"So you'd rather I lie to you?"

Trina laughs. "Just help me find something to wear to the prom, Miss Fashion Adviser."

"Since you asked . . ."

I pull out a sapphire blue gown marked down from $285 to $125. "This will look stunning on you," I tell Trina. "And with the empire waist, you won't have to worry about the baby weight. You should wear your hair up. You'll look fierce, I'm telling you."

Trina eyes the gown. "You really think so? I saw this on the rack but I thought it looked too plain."

"Try it on," I reply. "With dresses like this, you really have to see yourself in it. You'll be pleasantly surprised."

Trina strolls into the dressing room. Alyssa and I take a seat in the empty chairs nearby. Stacy pulls out a green dress so homely looking that I rush to my feet and snatch it out of her hands.

"Don't even think about it, girlfriend. I can't let you go to the prom looking all whack. You'll make the rest of us look bad."

Stacy laughs. "I was just looking at it."

I shake my head. "You don't even need to do that. This thing should be buried somewhere under a house or burned."

I stick it on a nearby rack.

Trina walks out of the dressing room.

"You look beautiful," Penny tells her.

"So what do you think, Miss Fashion Adviser?"

"I think Chance is going to love you in that dress. Make sure his bow tie and cummerbund match your gown."

Trina walks over and embraces me. "Thanks so much for helping me."

"You're welcome."

"You really think he's gonna like this dress?" Trina asks in a low whisper.

"If he doesn't, then my cousin is crazy."

After Trina pays for her dress, we decide to call it a day and have dinner together. We finish in time to meet Aunt Phoebe at the front entrance when she pulls up. She's surprised to see that Alyssa and I are empty-handed.

"The prom is special, Aunt Phoebe," I say. "We have to pick our dresses with care."

"Mom, we need to start looking immediately for the perfect prom dress," I tell her when she calls me later that evening. The prom is only five weeks away."

"My baby's first prom . . . I'm so excited for you. Baby girl, I can still remember my first prom."

"You have a great memory. That was such a looong time ago."

"Ha ha ha."

I laugh.

"So where do you want to look for a prom dress?"

"Mimi's getting her dress from this boutique in Hollywood called Prom Girl Couture. I've been to their website and those dresses are fierce. You can even design your own gown."

"I suppose Mimi's designing her gown for the prom," Mom says.

"Uh-huh. I saw a couple of dresses that I really liked on the site. Could you please take a look at them and tell me what you think?"

"Sure, I'll pull it up on my laptop right now."

I break into a grin. "Great."

After a few minutes, she says, "Okay, I'm here."

I direct her to the right page.

"Oh, Divine . . . I love this one. It's perfect for you."

"You don't think it's too much gold? I think the black-and-white one would look perfect on Alyssa."

"No, this is definitely the one for you. And you're right about the one for Alyssa. Have you shown it to her?"

"Not yet."

"Have her look at it. If you girls want them, we'll need to get the gowns ordered so that they'll be ready in time."

While we're on the internet, I have Mom visit the site where I found shoes that I think are absolutely perfect for the dress.

"You're right. They would be perfect for the gown." Mom orders the shoes without preamble. "What else do you need? Are you wearing gloves?"

"No, ma'am. I do need a purse though." I think it's pretty cool that even though Mom is in Canada filming a new movie, we can still shop together. I love her so much and we're getting closer every day.

She still gets on my last nerve when she goes into Mom mode, but I guess she can't help it. It's what parents do.

Madison calls me on my cell. I let it roll over to voice mail even though I have a feeling I'll be regretting it later if his selfish sister is home. I'm just not ready to get off the phone with my mom.

"I've been meaning to ask you about Mia. How is she doing?"

"Mom, she's moving to Atlanta soon. Her dad got a job there that pays a lot more money. But that's not the only reason. Her parents are scared that Tim might come back to hurt Mia."

"That might be the best thing for them to do. I'd certainly want you out of Temple if something like that was going on. It sounds like this boy was very violent."

"I feel so bad for keeping her secret as long as I did. If I'd said something sooner, she never would've gotten her arm broken. I was really trying to be a good friend."

"I know you were, baby girl, but I hope you understand that being a good friend means you don't keep secrets that can hurt the person."

"I get that now."

"Respect is the way to have a healthy relationship," Mom states. "Always remember that."

"You know what, Mom? I think God is the key to having a healthy relationship. Uncle Reed says God is love. That makes Him the expert, so we should always go to Him for wisdom, even when it comes to finding a boyfriend."

RESOURCES

Teachers, school counselors, school nurses

*Local rape crisis centers

*State domestic violence coalitions

*Local doctors and other health professionals

*Local psychologists and other mental health professionals

*Local police department

*Local shelters for battered women

Center for the Prevention of School Violence
1-800-299-6504

National Domestic Violence Hotline 1-800-799-SAFE

Rape, Abuse, and Incest National Network
1-800-656-HOPE

National Center for Victims of Crime
1-800-FYI-CALL
TTY: 1-800-211-7996

Care Net
1-800-395-HELP(4357)

National Child Abuse Hotline
1-800-4-A-CHILD
(1-800-422-4453)

Teen Helpline 1-800-400-0900

*Check your local phone book or consult with a school counselor, a close family member, or friend to help you find an organization near you.

Family Violence Prevention
Center 1-800-313-1310

National Organization for
Victim Assistance
1-800-TRYNOVA

National Resource Center
on Domestic Violence
1-800-537-2238

Covenant House Nine Line
1-800-999-9999

Healing Woman Foundation
1-800-477-4111

Youth Crisis Hotline
1-800-448-4663
1-800-422-0009

TeenLine 1-800-522-8336

WEBSITES

Break the Cycle
www.breakthecycle.org

See It & Stop It
www.seeitandstopit.org

Safe Network www.safenet
work.net/teens/teens.html

Love Is Not Abuse
www.loveisnotabuse.com
Liz Claiborne Inc. Initiative

When Love Hurts
www.dvirc.org.au/whenlove/

Relate for Teens Online
www.rippleeffects.com/
relateforteens/index.html

Teen Relationships Website
www.teenrelationships.org

U Have the Right
www.uhavetheright.net
Order the free CD:
U Have the Right, Volume 1

**Girls Inc. National Resource
Center** www.girlsinc.org

The Empower Program
www.empowered.org

Teen Central
www.teencentral.net

Prevent Violence
www.preventviolence.org

Reader's Group Guide for
divine secrets

Summary

In the latest installment of the *Divine* series, Divine Matthews-Hardison must figure out what being a friend really means. Divine is settling into life in rural Georgia, after her days as Hollywood's princess. She is getting used to the rules that her uncle Reed and aunt Phoebe have set, and she is building a stronger relationship with her mother.

Divine's cousin Alyssa is her closest friend, but her circle of friends continues to increase. Mia, a classmate, has been promoted to semi-best-friend. But, when Divine notices bruises on her friend Mia's arm, she wrongly assumes that her friend is being abused at home. Mia comes clean and confides it is actually her boyfriend, Tim, who has hurt her. Divine is torn between keeping Mia's secret and betraying Mia to keep her safe.

A Conversation with Jacquelin Thomas

Q. How has Divine's character evolved from the earlier books in the series, *Simply Divine* and *Divine Confidential*, to *Divine Secrets*?

A. She's settled comfortably into life in Temple, Georgia, and she's come into her own with her family. Away from public scrutiny and the media frenzy, she's just another teenager.

Q. **What made you decide to write** *Divine Secrets*? **What did you hope that readers would come away with after reading** *Divine Secrets*?

A. I'm very passionate when it comes to domestic violence, but when I saw the rising numbers of teens being abused, I felt I needed to address this issue. Love should never hurt, and that's the message I want to send across to my readers. And if *someone is* abusing you or you know of someone being abused—please tell. It could save a life.

Q. **Was there one person or several people that inspired the character of Divine Matthews-Hardison? Are there any characters that remind you of yourself?**

A. I think there's a little bit of me in each character. When I read or watch the news regarding the actions of celebrity parents, I often wonder what their children must think or how they must feel, and these questions inspired the series.

Q. **How does being a parent influence the adult roles you create in this novel?**

A. No parent is perfect and that includes me. I made some mistakes in parenting my own children, but I did the best I could with what I had to work with. My mother would say the same, as would her mother. We are parents through trial and error, and so are my adult characters. The one thing I do want to show in my books is that parents have to find a way to communicate with their children and vice versa.

Q. **You have had a long and diverse writing career starting with romance, moving to Christian adult novels, and now teen books. How is writing for teens different from writing your adult novels? What do you enjoy most?**

A. I enjoy writing! I love writing books that express my beliefs—this is also my ministry. I write to encourage, offer hope, and show that God is the answer to every problem in the world. I love writing for teens because they spend most of their teen years looking for answers. They are pressed with so much in the world and they need information on how to deal with life. It is my prayer that my books will give them some direction, but I want them to know that it's okay to be a Christian.

Q. **What do you do before writing your next novel?**

A. Vacation! My family and I just recently returned from a cruise to the Bahamas. We will be leaving in a few days for the beach. When I'm not writing, it's about the family. We're big football fans and my son plays, so we're gearing up for the upcoming season with football games every weekend.

Q. **What is your next teen book? Will it be another title in the *Divine* series?**

A. My next book in the *Divine* series is *Divine Match-up*. I'm very excited about this book and can't wait for it to hit the stores. Look for it in early 2008.

Q. **A good writer usually is a good reader. Who are your favorite authors? Which writers have influenced you the most?**

A. I'm a big mystery reader and I love James Patterson. I also love Michael Connelly, Alice Walker, Angela Benson, Pat G'Orge-Walker, and Shakespeare. There are lots more—too many to name. I basically love a good read.

Questions for Discussion

1. What are some of the ways that Chance and Trina's having a baby out of wedlock affect how Uncle Reed and Aunt Phoebe treat Divine and Alyssa? Do you think they are being too hard on the girls?

2. Trina and Chance have created a child together. Do you think they are ready to handle the responsibility? Use examples of their behavior in the book to explain your reasoning.

3. Alyssa tells Divine that Stephen asked her to have sex. She is afraid to say no because she does not want to break up with Stephen. Should Alyssa have confided in Divine? Do you think that Divine gave her good advice? Do you think Alyssa handled the situation well?

4. Divine and her mother are beginning to build a stronger bond, but Divine is uncomfortable with her mother's friend Kevin. Divine is afraid her mother's being in a relationship will lead Kara back to the destructive ways she had with Jerome. Is Divine being fair to her mother and Kevin? Do you think Kara is doing enough to help make Divine more comfortable with her and Kevin's relationship?

5. In *Divine Confidential* Madison broke up with Divine because she would not have sex with him. In this book, *Divine Secrets*, they get back together. Do you think Divine should have taken him back?

6. Why do you think Trina's parents won't let Chance take the baby overnight? Do you think they are right? How do you think Trina should respond to this situation?

7. Do you think that Divine is a good friend to Mia? Do you think Divine could have found another way to help Mia without telling her secret?

8. Often people are in abusive relationships and do not realize it because they think only of physical abuse. There is also emotional and sexual abuse. What kind of emotional abuse did Mia have to deal with while dating Tim?

9. Almost all of the teens in *Divine Secrets* have a boyfriend/girlfriend, and at some point they all seem to make a sacrifice (for example, Divine stays up late talking with Madison and is tired the next day). What are some of the other sacrifices made by characters to be in a relationship? Do you think it is worth it?

Activities to Enhance Your Book Club

1. Consider hosting a reading group with parents to discuss themes of the book.

2. Divine and Alyssa went shopping, and Divine realized that she could still find nice outfits without spending a great deal of money. Consider setting a challenge in which everyone would have to bring clippings for two full outfits that they would actually wear that are under a set amount of money.

3. Do some research on teenage dating abuse. Look into what teenagers can do to be more aware for themselves and friends. Find a way to spread the word about what you've learned. Dating rules and e-postcards can be found at www.chooserespect .org. Also check out the websites at the end of the book.

POCKET BOOKS
Proudly Presents

divine **match-up**

Coming in April 2008

"*Madison* and I got married last night," I announce to Alyssa as we're leaving the house to head to school.

Shocked and completely caught off guard, she nearly topples to the ground.

Trying to hold back a smile, I reach for Alyssa to keep her from falling and getting all embarrassed. Plus, it'll be hard for me to keep a straight face.

Straightening up, Alyssa says, *"You what?"*

"Girl, you heard me. Madison and I are married." I can hardly keep from cracking up in her face over the way she's standing there looking at me as if I'm wearing bright pink eye shadow or something not so cool. "I wish you could see the expression on your face right now."

Alyssa clearly doesn't believe me. "Divine, stop lying! First of all, you're only sixteen years old, and second, you were home last night with us. I know you didn't sneak out 'cause you're not crazy. You know my parents would chop your head off and mail it back to Los Angeles. By the way, April Fools' Day was yesterday."

She tries to be such a know-it-all sometimes, but I'm not about to let her faze me today. I'm in too good a mood. I'm on my honeymoon.

Some honeymoon. Going to school is not my idea of a romantic honeymoon. At least Madison and I have our nights in our private chat room.

"I can't believe you gon' try and lie about something like that," Alyssa fusses. "Like I'ma believe some stupid crap like that."

I navigate away from the house to make sure I'm out of earshot just in case Chance or Aunt Phoebe come outside. Alyssa's right about my aunt—she's straight crazy.

"This has nothing to do with April Fools' Day. Alyssa, I'm telling you the truth. Madison and I are married. We had a virtual wedding ceremony." I take out a piece of paper from my backpack. Handing it over to her, I say, "See . . . this is our wedding certificate. I told you. We're husband and wife."

"So how did you do it? How did you get married so quickly?" Alyssa asks, her dark brown eyes about to pop out of her head.

"There are several places on the web that will allow you to have a wedding, a reception—even a honeymoon suite. Madison and I have a suite for two weeks as part of our wedding package. You can get married for free on some sites, but, girl, you know me—I have to do it diva style so I paid fifty dollars for our wedding."

Alyssa gasps. "You paid fifty dollars? I would've just gotten married on one of the free ones."

"I wanted a nice wedding. Besides, it was only fifty dollars. That's really not a lot of money."

"Humph. It's still a lot of money to me." Alyssa's looking at me with that silly surprised expression on her face. "I can't believe you did it. You and Madison actually got married."

I keep glancing over my shoulder, making sure Chance isn't trying to sneak up on us. "Alyssa, you can't tell anyone. Madison and I are keeping it a secret."

"Girl, you better hope my parents don't hear about this. I know Mama will lose her mind if she finds out." Shaking her head in disbelief, Alyssa adds, "You the only person I know who skipped dating and went all the way to marriage. I guess you meant it when you said you don't half-step."

"I already know he's the person I want to be with, Alyssa. That's all dating is for—to find your Mr. Right. Well, I've done all that."

"If my parents find out, it'll be the only wedding you'll ever have," Alyssa warns. "Better enjoy it while you can."

"That's why you can't tell anyone. I don't want your parents to find out, and I especially don't want my mom to know."

"I'm not saying nothing," Alyssa vows. "But I do want to know what you and Madison plan on doing. Are you going to try and get your own apartment? Or are you going to keep your marriage a secret until you graduate?"

I stand there listening to Alyssa go on and on, biting back my laughter. She actually believes Madison and I are married for real. I decide to let her in on the real deal.

"Even if they do find out, it's not a real big deal. Alyssa, it's a game. We're role-playing. Our marriage isn't really legal."

Alyssa releases a short sigh of relief. "Girl, you had me thinking you were really married."

"We did have a ceremony performed by Preacher David at a cyber wedding chapel."

"Divine, how did you find out about this stuff? I've never heard of anybody getting married on the internet."

"You can find anything on the internet, Alyssa. I was on the internet looking up marriage ceremonies in different cultures for math and came across an article on online marriages in China. They call it *wanghun*. I was curious so I visited some websites for more information. I think it's pretty cool."

Alyssa frowns. "Why were you doing that for a math class?"

"We have to establish how weddings are celebrated in different cultures. Then we have to figure out the mathematical problems, like how many guests should be seated at a table if only eight tables are available, but ninety guests are expected to attend, or which food a person could buy for one hundred twenty-five guests if the budget's like a thousand dollars. Mr. Monroe doesn't have you all doing that?"

Alyssa shakes her head no. "Not yet anyway. But back to this wedding stuff. I've never heard of *waygum* . . . whatever you call it."

"It's pronounced *wang-hun*. I'm not surprised you haven't heard of it. It's not like you live in a *metropolis*." I'm thrilled to be able to use the word I'd learned just this morning from my word-of-the-day email.

"I know what that means," Alyssa brags, looking full of herself. "It means 'big city.' "

"You went and subscribed to Word.A.Day, didn't you?"

"Yeah, but I already knew what it meant. You're not the only smart one in the family."

We have about fifteen minutes to get to school before the first bell, so Alyssa and I pick up the pace. I'm hoping to see my *husband* before first period. Normally, I wear pants to school, but I'm wearing a new dress today just for him. Today is special.

Christian Novels for Teens!